Samuel French Acting Edition

In Darkest America

Tone Clusters

The Eclipse

I0591909

by Joyce Carol Oates

║SAMUEL FRENCH║

SAMUELFRENCH.COM   SAMUELFRENCH.CO.UK

FOR PRODUCTION ENQUIRIES

UNITED STATES AND CANADA
Info@SamuelFrench.com
1-866-598-8449

UNITED KINGDOM AND EUROPE
Plays@SamuelFrench.co.uk
020-7255-4302

Each title is subject to availability from Samuel French, depending
upon country of performance. Please be aware that *IN DARKEST
AMERICA* may not be licensed by Samuel French in your territory.
Professional and amateur producers should contact the nearest Samuel
French office or licensing partner to verify availability.

MUSIC USE NOTE

Licensees are solely responsible for obtaining formal written permission from copyright owners to use copyrighted music in the performance of this play and are strongly cautioned to do so. If no such permission is obtained by the licensee, then the licensee must use only original music that the licensee owns and controls. Licensees are solely responsible and liable for all music clearances and shall indemnify the copyright owners of the play(s) and their licensing agent, Samuel French, against any costs, expenses, losses and liabilities arising from the use of music by licensees. Please contact the appropriate music licensing authority in your territory for the rights to any incidental music.

IMPORTANT BILLING AND CREDIT REQUIREMENTS

If you have obtained performance rights to this title, please refer to your licensing agreement for important billing and credit requirements.

IN DARKEST AMERICA, two plays by Joyce Carol Oates, premiered at the 14th Annual Humana Festival of New American Plays March 8–April 7, 1990.

Tone Clusters was directed by Steven Albrezzi with the following cast (in order of appearance):

VOICE .... William McNulty
FRANK GULICK .... Peter Michael Goetz
EMILY GULICK .... Adale O'Brien

The Eclipse was also directed by Steven Albrezzi and had the following cast (in order of appearance):

STEPHANIE WASHBURN........... Beth Dixon
MURIEL WASHBURN..... Madeleine Sherwood
AILEEN STANLEY .... Gail Benedict
SEÑOR RíOS........................... Paul Rogers

TONE CLUSTERS

CHARACTERS

FRANK GULICK, 53 years old

EMILY GULICK, 51 years old

VOICE, Male, indeterminate age

These are white Americans of no unusual distinction, nor are they in any self-evident way "representative."

Tone Clusters is not intended to be a realistic work, thus any inclination toward the establishment of character should be resisted. Its primary effect should be visual (the dominance of the screen at center stage, the play of lights of sharply contrasting degrees of intensity) and audio (the VOICE, the employment of music—"tone clusters" of Henry Cowell and/or Charles Ives, and electronic music, etc.) The mood is one of fragmentation, confusion, yet, at times strong emotion. A fractured narrative emerges which the audience will have no difficulty piecing together even as—and this is the tragi-comedy of the piece—the characters Mr. and Mrs. Gulick deny it.

In structure, Tone Clusters suggests an interview, but a stylized interview in which questions and answers are frequently askew. Voices trail off into silence or may be mocked or extended by strands of music. The VOICE is sometimes overamplified and booming; sometimes marred by static; sometimes clear, in an ebullient tone, like that of a talk-show host. The VOICE has no identity but must be male. It should not be represented by any actual presence on the stage or within view of the audience. At all times, the VOICE is in control; the principals on the stage are dominated by their interrogator and by the screen which is seemingly floating in the air above them, at center stage. Indeed the screen emerges as a character.

The piece is divided into nine uneven segments. When one ends, the lights dim, then come up again immediately. (After the ninth segment lights go out completely and darkness is extended for some seconds to indicate that the piece is ended: it ends on an abrupt cut off of lights and images on screens.) By degree the Gulicks become somewhat accustomed to the experience of being interviewed and filmed, but never wholly accustomed; they are always slightly disoriented, awkward, confused, inclined to speak slowly and methodically or too quickly, "unprofessionally," often with inappropriate emotion (fervor, enthusiasm, hope, sudden rage) or no emotion at all (like "computer voices"). Gulicks may at times speak in unison (as if one were an echo of the other); they may mimic the qualities of tone cluster music or electronic music (I conceive of their voices, and that of the VOICE, as music of a kind); should the director wish, there may be some clear-cut relationship between subject and emotion or emphasis—but the piece should do no more than approach "realism," and then withdraw. The actors must conceive of themselves as elements in a dramatic structure, not as "human characters" wishing to establish rapport with an audience.

Tone Clusters is about the absolute mystery—the *not-knowing*—at the core of our human experience. That the mystery is being exploited by a television documentary underscores its tragi-comic nature.

Scene 1

LIGHTS UP. Initially very strong, near-blinding. On a bare stage, middle-aged FRANK and EMILY GULICK sit ill-at-ease in "comfortable" modish cushioned swivel chairs, trying not to squint or grimace in the lights (Which may be represented as the lights of a camera crew provided the human figures involved can be kept shadowy, even indistinct). THEY wear clip-on microphones to which they are unaccustomed. THEY are "dressed up" for the occasion, and clearly nervous: THEY continually touch their faces, or clasp their hands firmly in their laps, or fuss with fingernails, buttons, the microphone cords, their hair. The nervous mannerisms continue throughout the piece but should never be too distracting and never comic.

Surrounding the Gulicks, dominating their human presence, are t.v. monitors and/or slide screens upon which, during the course of the play, disparate images, words, formless flashes of light are projected. Even when the Gulicks' own images appear on the screens they are upstaged by it: THEY glance at it furtively, with a kind of awe.

The monitors always show the stage as we see it: the GULICKS seated, glancing uneasily up at the screen. Thus there is a "screen-within-a-screen."

The employment of music is entirely at the director's discretion. The opening might be accompanied by classical tone cluster piano pieces—Henry Cowell's "Advertisement" for instance. The MUSIC should never be intrusive. The ninth scene might well be completely

empty of music. There should certainly be no "film-music" effect. (The GULICKS do not hear the music.)
The VOICE too in its modulations is at the discretion of the director. In a way, I would like Tone Clusters to be aleatory, but that might prove too radical for practicality. Certainly at the start the VOICE is booming and commanding. There should be intermittent audio trouble (WHISTLING, STATIC, etc.); the VOICE, wholly in control, can exude any number of effects throughout the play—pomposity, charity, condescension, bemusement, false chattiness, false pedantry, false sympathy, mild incredulity (like that of a television m.c.), affectless "computer talk." The GULICKS are entirely intimidated by the VOICE and try very hard to answer its questions.
SCREEN shifts from its initial image to words: IN A CASE OF MURDER—large black letters on white.

VOICE. In a case of murder (taking murder as an abstraction)   there is always a sense of the inevitable once the identity of the murderer is established. Beforehand there is a sense of disharmony.

And humankind fears and loathes disharmony, Mr. and Mrs. Gulick of Lakepointe, New Jersey would you comment?

FRANK. ... Yes I would say,   I think that

EMILY. What is that again, exactly?   I ...

FRANK. My wife and I, we ...

EMILY. Disharmony ...?

FRANK. I don't like disharmony.   I mean, all the family, we are a law-abiding family.

VOICE. A religious family   I believe?

FRANK. Oh yes.   Yes,
We go to church every

EMILY. We almost never miss a,   a Sunday

For a while,   I helped with Sunday School classes
The children,   the children don't always go but they
believe, our daughter Judith for instance she   and Carl
FRANK. oh yes yessir.
EMILY. and Dennis,   they do believe they were raised
to   believe in God and, and Jesus Christ
FRANK. We raised them that way because   we were
raised that way,
EMILY. there *is* a God whether you agree with Him
or not.
VOICE. "Religion" may be defined as   a sort of
adhesive matter invisibly holding together   nation-states,
nationalities, tribes, families   for   the   good   of
those   so   held together,   would you
comment?
FRANK. Oh,   oh yes.
EMILY. For the good of ...
FRANK. Yes I would say so,   I think so.
EMILY. My husband and I, we were married in church,
in
FRANK. In the Lutheran Church.
EMILY. In Penns Neck.
FRANK. In New Jersey.
EMILY. All our children,
BOTH. they believe.
EMILY. God sees into the human heart.
VOICE. Mr. and Mrs. Gulick   from your experience
would you   theorize for our audience: is the Universe
"predestined"   in every particular   or   is   man
capable   of   acts of   "freedom"?
BOTH. ...
EMILY. ... I would say,   that is hard to say.
FRANK. Yes. I believe that man is free.
EMILY. If you mean like, I guess   choosing good
and evil?   Yes

FRANK. I would have to say   yes. You would have to say   mankind is free.

FRANK. Like moving my hand. (*Moves hand.*)

EMILY. If nobody is free   it wouldn't be right would it   to punish anybody?

FRANK. There is always   Hell.

I believe in Hell.

EMILY. Anybody at all

FRANK. Though I am not free to, to   fly up in the air am I? (*Laughs.*) because   Well I'm not built right for that am I? (*Laughs.*)

VOICE. Man is free.   Thus man is   responsible for his acts.

EMILY. Except, oh   sometime if,   maybe for instance if

A baby born without

FRANK. Oh one of those "AIDS" babies

EMILY. Poor thing

FRANK. "crack" babies

Or if you were captured   by some enemy, y'know and tortured

Some people never have a chance,

EMILY. But God sees into the human heart,

God knows who to forgive   and who not.

(*LIGHTS down.*)

Scene 2

Screen shows a suburban street of lower-income homes; the GULICKS stare at the screen and their answers are initially distracted.

VOICE. Here we have Cedar Street   in Lakepointe,
New Jersey   neatly kept homes (as you can see)
American suburb   low crime rate, single-family homes
suburb of Newark, New Jersey   population 12,000
the neighborhood of Mr. and Mrs. Frank Gulick the parents
of   Carl Gulick. Will you introduce yourselves to our
audience please?

(*HOUSELIGHTS come up.*)

FRANK. ... Go on, you first
EMILY. I, I don't know what to say
FRANK. My name is   Frank Gulick, I   I am fifty-
three years old   that's our house there   2368 Cedar
Street
EMILY. My name is Emily Gulick, fifty-one years old,
VOICE. How employed,   would you care to say?
Mr. Gulick?
FRANK. I work for the post office,   I'm a supervisor
for
EMILY. He has worked for the post office for twenty-
five years
FRANK. ... The Terhune Avenue Branch.
VOICE. And how long have you resided   in your
attractive home   on Cedar Street?

(*HOUSELIGHTS begin to fade down.*)

FRANK. ... Oh I guess, how long   if this is
this is 1990?
EMILY. (oh just think: 1990!)
FRANK. we moved there in, uh   Judith wasn't born
yet so
EMILY. Oh there was our thirtieth anniversary a year
ago,

FRANK. wedding
no that was two years ago
EMILY. was it?
FRANK. or three, I   twenty-seven years, this is 1990
EMILY. Yes: Judith is twenty-six,   now I'm a
grandmother
FRANK. Carl is twenty-two
EMILY. Denny is seventeen, he's a senior in high
school
No none of them are living at home now
FRANK. not now
EMILY. Right now poor Denny is staying with my
sister in
VOICE. Frank and Emily Gulick you have been happy
here   in Lakepointe raising your family like any
American couple   with your hopes and aspirations
until recently?
FRANK. ... Yes, oh yes.
EMILY. Oh for a long time we *were*
FRANK. oh yes.
EMILY. It's so strange to,   to think of
The years go by so
VOICE. You have a   happy family life like so many
millions   of Americans
EMILY. Until this, this terrible thing
FRANK. *Innocent until proven guilty*—that's a laugh!
EMILY. Oh it's a, a terrible thing
FRANK. Never any hint beforehand of   the
meanness of people's hearts.
I mean the neighbors.
EMILY. Oh now don't start that, this isn't the
FRANK. Oh God you just try to comprehend
EMILY. this isn't the place, I
FRANK. Like last night: this carload of kids
drunk, beer-drinking foul language in the night

EMILY. oh don't, my hands are

FRANK. Yes but you know it's the parents set them going   And telephone calls   our number is changed now, but

EMILY. my hands are shaking so

we are both on medication   the doctor says,

FRANK. oh you would not believe, you would not believe the hatred like Nazi Germany

EMILY. Denny had to drop out of school,   he loved school he is an honor student

FRANK. everybody turned against us

EMILY. My sister in Yonkers, he's staying with

FRANK. Oh he'll never be the same   boy again, none of us will.

VOICE. In the development of   human identity there's the element of chance,   and there is genetic determinism.

Would you comment please?

FRANK. The thing is,   you try your best.

EMILY. oh dear God yes.

FRANK. Your best.

EMILY. You give all that's in your heart

FRANK. you

can't do more than that can you?

EMILY. Yes but there is certain to be   justice.

There *is* a, a sense of things.

FRANK. Sometimes there is a chance, the way they turn out

but also   what they *are*.

EMILY. Your own babies

VOICE. Frank Gulick and Mary   what is your assessment of

American civilization   today?

EMILY. ...It's Emily.

FRANK. My wife's name is,

EMILY. It's
Emily.
VOICE. Frank and EMILY   Gulick.
FRANK. ... The state of the   civilization?
EMILY. It's so big,
FRANK. We are here to tell our side of,
EMILY. ... I don't know: it's a,   a Democracy
FRANK. the truth is,   do you want the truth?
the truth is where we live
Lakepointe it's changing too
EMILY. it has changed
FRANK. Yes but it's all over, it's
terrible, just terrible
EMILY. Now we are grandparents we fear for
FRANK. Yes what you read and see on t.v.
EMILY. You don't know what to think,
FRANK. Look: in this country   half the crimes
are committed by the,   by half the population against
the other half. (*Laughs.*)
You have your law-abiding citizens,
EMILY. taxpayers
FRANK. and you have the rest of them.
Say you went downtown into a city like   Newark,
some night
EMILY. you'd be crazy if you got out of your car
FRANK. you'd be dead.   That's what.
VOICE. Is it possible,   probable   or in your
assessment *im*probable that the slaying of   fourteen-
year-old   Edith Kaminsky   on February 12, 1990
is related to
the social malaise   of which you speak?
FRANK. ... "ma-lezz"?
EMILY. ... oh it's hard to,   I would say yes
FRANK. ... whoever did it, he
EMILY. Oh it's terrible the things that

keep happening
FRANK. If only the police would arrest the right
person,
    VOICE. Frank and Emily Gulick   you remain
adamant in your belief   in your faith in your
twenty-two-year-old son   Carl
    that he is innocent   in the death of   fourteen-
year-old Edith Kaminsky
    on February 12, 1990?
    EMILY. Oh yes,
    FRANK. oh yes that is the single thing we are
convinced of.
    EMILY. On this earth.
    BOTH. With God as our witness,
    FRANK. yes
    EMILY. Yes.
    FRANK. The single thing.

(LIGHTS down).

Scene 3

*LIGHTS up. SCREEN shows violent movement: urban
scenes, police patrol cars, a fire burning out of control,
men being arrested and herded into vans; a body lying in
the street. The GULICKS stare at the screen.*

    VOICE. Of today's pressing political issues   the rise
in violent crime most concerns American citizens
Number one political issue of   Mr. and Mrs. Gulick
tell our viewers your opinion?
    FRANK. In this state
    the state of New Jersey
    EMILY. Oh it's everywhere
    FRANK. there's capital punishment supposedly

EMILY. But the lawyers   the lawyers get them off,
FRANK. you bet
There's public defenders the taxpayer pays
EMILY. Oh, it's   it's out of control
(like that what is it "acid rain")
FRANK. It can fall on you anywhere,
EMILY. the sun is too hot too:
BOTH. (the "greenhouse effect")
FRANK. It's a welfare state by any other name
EMILY. Y'know who pays:
BOTH. the taxpayer
FRANK. The same God damn criminal, you pay for
him   then he
That's the joke of it (*Laughs.*)
the same criminal who slits your throat (*Laughs.*)
He's the one you pay bail for to get out.
But it sure isn't funny. (*Laughs.*)
EMILY. Oh God.
FRANK. It sure isn't funny.
VOICE. Many Americans have come to believe   this
past decade   that capital punishment is one of the
answers: would you comment please?
FRANK. Oh in cases of actual, proven   murder
EMILY. Those drug dealers
FRANK. Yes *I* would have to say, definitely   yes
EMILY. I would say so yes
FRANK. You always hear them say   opponents of
the death penalty
"The death penalty doesn't stop crime"
EMILY. Oh that's what they say!
FRANK. Yes but *I* say, once a man is dead he sure isn't
gonna commit any more crimes, is he. (*Laughs.*)
VOICE. The death penalty *is* a deterrent to crime   in
those cases
when the criminal has been   executed

FRANK. But you have to find the right,
the actual murderer.
EMILY. Not some poor innocent   some poor
innocent.[*]

(LIGHTS down.)

Scene 4

*LIGHTS up. SCREEN shows a grainy magnified snapshot
of a boy about ten. Quick jump to a snapshot of the
same boy a few years older. Throughout this scene
images of "CARL GULICK" appear and disappear on
the screen though not in strict relationship to what is
being said, nor in chronological order. "CARL
GULICK" in his late teens and early twenties is
muscular but need not have any other outstanding
characteristics: he may look like any American boy at
all.*

VOICE. Carl Gulick, twenty-two years old   the
second-born child of Frank and Emily Gulick   of
Lakepoint, New Jersey   How would you describe your
son, Frank and Emily
FRANK. D'you mean how he looks or ...?
EMILY. He's a shy boy, he's shy   Not backward just
FRANK. He's about my height I guess   brown hair,
eyes
EMILY. Oh! no I think   he's much taller Frank
he's been taller than you   for years

---

[*] "Innocent" is an adjective here, not a noun.

FRANK. Well that depends on how we're both
standing.
How we're both   standing
Well in one newspaper it said six feet one inch, in the
other
    six feet three inches, that's the kind of
EMILY. accuracy
FRANK. reliability of the news media
you can expect!
EMILY. And oh that terrible picture of,
in the paper
that face he was making   the police carrying him
against his will   laying their hands on him
FRANK. handcuffs
EMILY. Oh that isn't *him*
BOTH. that isn't our son

(*GULICKS respond dazedly to snapshots flashed on
    screen.*)

EMILY. Oh! that's Carl   age I guess about
FRANK. four?
EMILY. that's at the beach one summer
FRANK. only nine or ten, he was big for
EMILY. With his sister Judith
FRANK. that's my brother George
EMILY. That's
FRANK. he loved Boy Scouts,
EMILY. but
Oh when you are the actual parents it's a different
FRANK. Oh it is so different!
from something just on t.v.
VOICE. In times of disruption   of fracture   it
is believed that human behavior moves   in unchartable

leaps   History is a formal record of such   leaps   but
in large-scale demographical   terms
     in which the   individual   is   lost
     Frank and Emily Gulick it's said your son   Carl
charged in the savage slaying of   fourteen-year-old
shows no sign of   remorse   that is to say,
awareness of the act: thus the question we pose to you
Can guilt reside in those   devoid of "memory"
     EMILY. ... Oh the main thing is,
     he is innocent.
     FRANK. ... Stake my life on it.
     EMILY. He has always been   cheerful, optimistic
     FRANK. a good boy, of course he has not
     forgotten
     BOTH. He is innocent.
     EMILY. How could our son "forget" when he has
nothing to
     BOTH. "forget"
     FRANK. He took that lie detector test voluntarily didn't
he
     EMILY. Oh there he is   weight-lifting, I don't
remember
     who took that picture?
     FRANK. When you are the actual parents you see them
every day,
     you don't form judgments.
     VOICE. In every household in America   albums of
family
     lovingly preserved,   many Baby Books of course
Those without children elect to have   pets: a billion-
dollar industry
     Many young people of our time   faced   with
rising costs in   housing   prefer to remain in the
parental   home

And how is your son employed, Mr. and Mrs.
Kaminsky?

Excuse me: GULICK.

FRANK. Up until Christmas he was working in
This butcher shop in East Orange

EMILY. ... it isn't easy, at that age

FRANK. Before that, loading and unloading

EMILY. at Sears at the mall

FRANK. No: that was before, that was before the other

EMILY. No: the job at Sears was

FRANK. ... Carl was working for that Italian, y'know
that

EMILY. the lawn service

FRANK. Was that before?   or after

Oh in this butcher shop   his employer

EMILY. yes there were hard feelings, on both sides

FRANK. Look: you can't believe a single thing   in
the newspaper or t.v.

EMILY. it's not that they lie

FRANK. Oh yes they lie

EMILY. not that they lie, they just   get everything
wrong

FRANK. Oh they do lie!   And it's printed and you
can't stop them.

EMILY. In this meat shop, I never wanted him to work
there

FRANK. In this shop there was pressure on him
to join the union.

EMILY. Then the other side, his employer
did not want him to join.

He's a sensitive boy,   his stomach and nerves

He lost his appetite for weeks, he'd say "oh if you could
see

some of the things I see"   "the insides of things"
and so much blood

VOICE. There was always a loving   relationship
in the household?

EMILY. ... When they took him away he said,   he
was so brave
he said Momma I'll be back soon
I'll be right back,   I am innocent he said
I don't know how she came to be in   our house
I don't know,   I don't know he said
I looked into my son's eyes and saw   truth shining
His eyes have always been   dark green,
like mine.

VOICE. On the afternoon of   February 12 you have
told police that
no one was home   in your house?

EMILY. I, I was ... I had a doctor's appointment,
My husband was working, he doesn't get home until

FRANK. Whoever did it,   and brought her body in

EMILY. No: they say she was   they say it,   it
happened there

FRANK. No I don't buy that,   He brought her in
carried her
whoever that was,
I believe he tried   other houses
seeing who was home and who   wasn't
and then he

EMILY. Oh it was like lightning striking

VOICE. Your son Dennis   was at Lakepointe High
School attending a meeting of the yearbook staff,   your
son Carl has told police he
was   riding   his motor scooter
in the park,

FRANK. They dragged him like   an animal
put their hands on him like
Like Nazi Germany,

EMILY. it couldn't be any worse

FRANK. And that judge
it's a misuse of power, it's
EMILY. I just don't understand.
VOICE. Your son Carl on and after   February 12
did not exhibit (in your presence)   any unusual sign of
emotion?
agitation?   guilt?
EMILY. Every day in a house,   a household
is like the other days.   Oh you never step back, never
see.
Like I told them, the   police,   everybody. *He did
not*.

(*LIGHTS down.*)

Scene 5

*LIGHTS up. SCREEN shows snapshots, photographs of
the murdered girl KAMINSKY. Like Carl Gulick, she
is anyone of that age: white: neither strikingly beautiful
nor unattractive.*

VOICE. Sometime in the evening of February 12 of
this year forensic reports say   fourteen-year-old Edith
Kaminsky daughter of   neighbors 2361 Cedar Street,
Lakepointe, New Jersey   multiple stab wounds, sexual
assault   strangulation
An arrest has been made but   legally or otherwise,
the absolute identity of the murderer has yet to be
EMILY. Oh it's so unjust,
FRANK. the power of a single man
That judge
EMILY. Carl's birthday is   next week

Oh God he'll be in that terrible   cold place
FRANK. "segregated" they call it
How can a judge refuse to set bail
EMILY. oh I would borrow a million dollars
if I could
FRANK. Is this America or   Russia?
EMILY. I can't stop crying
FRANK. ... we are both under medication you see but
EMILY. Oh it's true he wasn't himself   sometimes.
FRANK. But that day when it happened, that wasn't
one of the times.
VOICE. You hold out for the possibility that   the
true murderer   carried Edith Kaminsky into your house,
into your basement
thus meaning to throw suspicion on your son?
FRANK. Our boy is guiltless that's the main thing, I
will never doubt that.
EMILY. Our body is innocent ...   What did I say?
FRANK. Why the hell do they make so much of
Carl lifting weights, his   muscles
He is not a freak.
EMILY. There's lots of them   and women too, today
like that,
FRANK. He has other interests he used to collect
stamps   play baseball
EMILY. Oh there's so much misunderstanding
FRANK. actual lies
Because the police do not know who the murderer *is*
of course they will blame   anyone they can.

(*LIGHTS down.*)

Scene 6

*LIGHTS up. SCREEN shows the exterior of the Gulick
house seen from various angles; then, the interior (the
basement, evidently, and the "storage area" where the
young girl's body was found).*

VOICE. If, as believed, "premeditated" acts arise   out
of a mysterious sequence of neuron discharges   (in the
brain) out of what source   do

"unpremeditated"   acts   arise?

EMILY. Nobody was down in,   in the basement
until the police came.   The storage space is behind
the water heater,   but

FRANK. My God if my son is   so shiftless   like
people are saying just look: he helped me paint the house
last summer

EMILY. Yes Carl and Denny both,

FRANK. Why are they telling such   lies, our
neighbors?   We have never wished them harm,

EMILY. I believed a certain neighbor was my friend,
her and I, we we'd go shopping together   took my car
Oh my heart is broken

FRANK. It's robin's-egg blue,   the paint turned
out brighter than
when it dried, a little brighter than we'd
expected

EMILY. *I* think it's pretty

FRANK. Well.   We'll have to sell the house,   there's
no choice
the legal costs   Mr. Filco our attorney has said

EMILY. He told us

FRANK. he's going to fight all the way, he believes
Carl is   innocent

EMILY. My heart is broken.

FRANK. *My* heart isn't,
I'm going to fight this all the way
EMILY. A tragedy like this,   you learn fast
who is your friend and who is your enemy
FRANK. Nobody's your friend.
VOICE. The Gulicks and Kaminskys were   well
acquainted?
EMILY. We lived on Cedar first,   when they moved
in I don't remember:
my mind isn't right these days
FRANK. Oh yes   we knew them
EMILY. I'd have said Mrs. Kaminsky   was my
friend, but
that's how people are
FRANK. Yes
EMILY. Carl knew her,   Edith
I mean, we all did
FRANK. but not well,
EMILY. just neighbors
Now they're our declared enemies, the Kaminskys
FRANK. well,   so be it.
EMILY. Oh! that poor girl   if only she hadn't,
I mean, there's no telling who   she was with,
walking home
walking home from school I guess
FRANK. Well she'd been missing overnight,
EMILY. yes overnight
FRANK. Of course we were aware
FRANK. The Kaminskys came around ringing
doorbells,
EMILY. then the police,
FRANK. then
they got a search party going,   Carl helped them out
EMILY. Everybody said how much he helped
FRANK. he kept at it for hours

They walked miles and miles,
he's been out of work for a while,
EMILY. he'd been looking
in the *help wanted* ads but
FRANK. ... He doesn't like to use the telephone.
EMILY. People laugh at him he says,
FRANK. I told him no he was imagining it.
EMILY. This neighborhood:
FRANK. you would not believe it.
EMILY. Call themselves Christians
FRANK. Well,   some are Jews
EMILY. Well it's still white isn't it   a white
neighborhood,   you expect better.
VOICE. The murder weapon   has yet to be found?
FRANK. One of the neighbors had to offer an opinion,
something sarcastic I guess
Oh don't go into *that*
FRANK. the color of the paint   on our house
So Carl said, You don't like it, wear sunglasses.
EMILY. But,
he was smiling.
VOICE. A young man with a sense of   humor.
FRANK. Whoever hid that poor girl's
body
in the storage space of our,
basement well clearly it
obviously it was   to deceive
to cast blame on our son.
EMILY. Yes   if there were fingerprints down there,
BOTH. that handprint they found on the wall
FRANK. well for God's sake it was from when Carl
was down there
BOTH. helping them
FRANK. He cooperated with them,
EMILY. Frank wasn't home,

FRANK. Carl led them downstairs
EMILY. Why they came to our house, I don't know.
Who was saying things   I don't know,
it was like everybody had gone   crazy
casting blame on all sides
VOICE. Mr. and Mrs. Gulick   it's said that from
your son's room
      Lakepointe police officers confiscated   comic books,
military magazines, pornographic magazines   a cache of
more than one dozen
      knives including   switchblades   plus
      a U.S. Army bayonet (World War II)
      Nazi memorabilia including a "souvenir" S.S. helmet
(manufactured in Taiwan)
      a pink plastic skull   with light bulbs in eyes
      a naked Barbie doll,   badly scratched
      numerous pictures of naked women
      and women in magazines,
      their eyes   breasts   crotches   cut out with a
scissors
      Do you have any comment   Mr. and Mrs. Gulick?
FRANK. Mainly they were hobbies,
EMILY. I guess I don't,
FRANK. we didn't know about
EMILY. Well   he wouldn't allow me in his room,
to vacuum or anything
FRANK. You know how boys are.
EMILY. Didn't want his mother
FRANK. poking her nose in
EMILY. So ... (*EMILY upsets glass of water.*)
      VOICE. Police forensic findings   (bloodstains, hairs,
semen)   and the DNA "fingerprinting"   constitute a
tissue of circumstance   linking your son to the murder
but cannot rise   to revelation?
      EMILY. Mr. Filco says   it's all pieced together

Circumstantial evidence, he says.

FRANK. *I* call it bullshit. (*Laughs.*)

EMILY. Oh Frank

FRANK. *I* call it bullshit. (*Laughs.*)

VOICE. Eye witnesses seem to   disagree,   two parties report having seen Carl Gulick and   Edith Kaminsky   walking together in the afternoon, but a third party   a neighbor   claims to have seen the girl in the company of a stranger   at approximately 4:15 pm

And Carl Gulick insists he was riding his motor scooter all that afternoon.

FRANK. He is a boy

EMILY. not capable of lying.

FRANK. Look: I would discipline him sometimes,

EMILY. you have to, with boys

FRANK. Oh yes you have to, otherwise

EMILY. He was always a good eater

FRANK. He's a quiet boy

EMILY. you can't guess his thoughts

FRANK. But he loved his mother and father

EMILY. always well behaved at home.

That ugly picture of him in the paper,

FRANK. that wasn't him.

EMILY. You can't believe the cruelty in the human heart.

FRANK. Giving interviews

EMILY. telling such cruel lies

FRANK. his own teachers from high school

VOICE. Mr. and Mrs. Gulick you had no suspicion no awareness   you had no sense of   the fact that   the battered and mutilated body of

fourteen-year-old Edith Kaminsky

VOICE. was hidden in your basement   in a storage space

wrapped in plastic garbage bags

for approximately   forty hours,
no   consciousness of   any disharmony   in
your household?
EMILY. Last week at my sister's where we were
staying,
we had to leave   this terrible place
in Yonkers I was crying,   I could not stop   crying
downstairs in the kitchen   three in the morning
I was standing by a window and there was suddenly   it
looked like snow!
it was moonlight moving in the window and there came
a   shadow I guess
like an eclipse?   was there an eclipse?
Oh I felt so, I felt   my heart stopped   Oh but I, I
wasn't scared
I was thinking   I was seeing how the world is
how the universe *is*
it's so hard to say, I feel like a   a fool
I was gifted by this, by   seeing   how the world *is*
not
how you see it   with your eyes, or talk   talk about it
I mean names you give to,   parts of it   No I mean
how it *is*
when there is nobody there.
VOICE. A subliminal conviction of disharmony
may be nullified by   a transcendental leap of
consciousness;   to a "higher plane"
of celestial harmony,
would you comment   Mr. and Mrs. Gulick?
EMILY. Then Sunday night it was,
FRANK. this last week
EMILY. they came again
FRANK. threw trash on our lawn
EMILY. screamed

Murderers! they were drunk, yelling   in the night
Murderers!

FRANK. There was the false report that Carl was
released on   bail

that he was home with us,

EMILY. Oh dear God if only that was true

FRANK. I've lost fifteen pounds since February

EMILY. Oh Frank has worked so hard   on that lawn,

it's his pride and joy and in the neighborhood
everybody knows, they compliment him,   and now

Yes he squats right out there, he pulls out crabgrass
by hand

Dumping such ugly nasty disgusting things

Then in the A&P a woman followed me   up and
down the aisles I could hear people   *That's her, that's the
mother of the murderer*   I could hear them   everywhere
in the store *Is that her,   is that the mother of the
murderer?*   they were saying   Lived in this
neighborhood, in this town   for so many years we
thought we were welcome here and now

Aren't you ashamed to show your face!   a voice
screamed

What can I do with my face,   can I hide it forever?

FRANK. And all this when our boy is   innocent.

VOICE. Perceiving the inviolate nature of   the
Universe   apart from human suffering   rendered you
happy, Mrs. Gulick   is this so?

for some precious moments?

EMILY. Oh yes, I was crying but
not because of
no   I was crying because
I was happy I think.

(*LIGHTS down.*)

Scene 7

LIGHTS up. SCREEN shows neurological X-rays, medical diagrams, charts as of EEG and CAT-scan tests.

VOICE. Is it possible that in terms of   fracture, of evolutionary unease   or, perhaps, at any time   human behavior mimics that of minute   particles   of light? The atom is primarily emptiness   the neutron dense-packed
The circuitry of the human brain   circadian rhythms can be tracked but never,   it's said comprehended. And then   in descent from "identity" (memory?)   to tissue to cells to cell-particles   electrical impulses axon-synapse-dendrite   and beyond, beneath
to sub-atomic bits
Where is "Carl Gulick"?

(GULICKS turn to each other in bewilderment. SCREEN flashes images: kitchen interior; weight-lifting paraphernalia; a shelf of trophies; photographs; domestic scenes, etc.)

VOICE. Mr. and Mrs. Gulick you did not notice anything   unusual   in your son's behavior on the night of February 12   or the following day,   to the best   of your recollection?
EMILY. ... Oh we've told the police this so many many times
FRANK. Oh you forget what you remember,
EMILY. That night, before we knew there was anyone missing   I mean, in the neighborhood   anyone we knew

FRANK. I can't remember.

EMILY. Yes but Carl had supper with us like always

FRANK. No I think,   he was napping up in his room

EMILY. he was at the table with us:

FRANK. I remember   he came down around nine o'clock,   but he did eat.

EMILY. Him and Denny, they were at the table with us

FRANK. We've told the police this so many times, it's I don't know any longer

EMILY. I'm sure it was Denny too.   Both our sons. We had meatloaf   ketchup baked on top, it's the boys' favorite dish just about   isn't it?

FRANK. Oh anything with hamburger and ketchup!

EMILY. Of course he was at the table with us,   he had his usual appetite.

FRANK. ... he was upstairs, said he had a touch of flu

EMILY. Oh no he was there.

FRANK. It's hard to speak of your own flesh and blood,   as if   they are other people

it's

hard   without giving false testimony against your will.

VOICE. Is the intrusion of the "extra-ordinary"   into the dimension of the "ordinary"   an indication that such Aristotellan categories are invalid?   If one day fails to resemble the preceding   what does it resemble?

FRANK. ... He has sworn to us, we are his parents

He did not touch a hair of that poor child's head   let alone the rest.

Anybody who knew him, they'd know

EMILY. Oh those trophies!   he was so proud

one of them is from the, I guess the Lakepointe YMCA

there's some from the New Jersey competition   at Atlantic City two years ago?

FRANK. no, he was in high school
the first was, Carl was only fifteen years old
EMILY. Our little muscle-man!
VOICE. Considering the evidence of thousands of years
of human culture of language   art   religion   the
judicial system   "The family unit"   athletics
hobbies   fraternal organizations   charitable impulses
gods of all species   is   it   possible   that
humankind   desires
    not   to   know
    its   place   in
    the
    food cycle?
EMILY. One day he said   he wasn't going back to
school,
    my heart was broken.
FRANK. Only half his senior year ahead
but you can't argue,   not with
EMILY. oh his temper!   he takes after,
oh I don't know who
FRANK. we always have gotten along together
in this household   haven't we
EMILY. yes but the teachers would laugh at him he
said
    girls laughed at him he said   stared and pointed at
him he said
    and there was this pack of   oh we're not prejudiced
against Negroes,   it's just that
    the edge of the Lakepointe school district
    well
FRANK. Carl got in fights sometimes
in the school cafeteria and   I guess the park?
EMILY. the park isn't safe for law-abiding people these
days
    they see the color of your skin,   they'll attack

some of them are just like animals   yes they *are*

FRANK. Actually our son was attacked first   it isn't like he got   into fights by himself

EMILY. Who his friends are now, I don't remember

FRANK. He is a quiet boy, keeps to himself

EMILY. he wanted to work

he was looking for work

FRANK. Well: our daughter Judith was misquoted about that

EMILY. also about Carl having a bad temper   she never said that

the reporter for the paper twisted her words

Mr. Filco says   we might sue

FRANK. Look: our son never raised a hand against anybody let alone against

EMILY. He loves his mother and father,   he respects us

FRANK. He is a religious boy at heart

EMILY. He looked me in the eyes he said Momma you believe me don't you?   and I said Oh yes Oh yes   he's just my baby

FRANK. nobody knows him

EMILY. nobody knows him the way we do

FRANK. who would it be, if they did?

I ask you.

(*HOUSELIGHTS come up, t.v. screen shows video rewind. SOUNDS of audio rewind. SCREEN shows GULICKS onstage.*)

VOICE. Frank and Mary Gulick we're very sorry something happened to the tape we're going to have to reshoot   Let's go back just to, we're showing an

interior   Carl's room   the trophies Ill say, I'll be repeating
    Are you ready?

(*HOUSELIGHTS out, all tech returns to normal.*)

VOICE. Well Mr. and Mrs. Gulick your son has quite a collection of trophies!
FRANK. ... I,   I don't remember what I
EMILY. ... yes he,
FRANK. Carl was proud of   he had other hobbies though
EMILY. Oh he was so funny, didn't want his mother poking through his room   he said
FRANK. Yes but that's   how boys are
EMILY. That judge refuses to set bail, which I don't understand
FRANK. Is this the United States or   is this the Soviet Union?
EMILY. we are willing to sell our house to stand up for what is
VOICE. You were speaking of your son Carl having quit school,
    his senior year?   and then?
EMILY. ... He had a hard time, the teachers   were down on him.
FRANK. I don't know why,
EMILY. we were never told
And now in the newspapers
FRANK. the kinds of lies they are saying
EMILY. that he got into fights, that he was
FRANK. that kind of thing is all a distortion
EMILY. He was always a quiet boy
FRANK. but he had his own friends

EMILY. they came over to the house sometime, I don't remember   who

FRANK. there was that one boy what was his name

EMILY. Oh Frank   Carl hasn't seen him in years he had friends in grade school

FRANK. Look: in the newspaper there were false statements

EMILY. Mr. Filco says   we might sue

FRANK. Oh no: he says we can't,   we have to prove "malice"

EMILY. Newspapers and t.v. are filled with lies

FRANK. Look: our son Carl never raised a hand against anybody let alone against

EMILY. He loves his mother and father,

FRANK. He respects us

VOICE. Frank and,   it's Emily isn't it   Frank and Emily Gulick

that is very moving.

(*LIGHTS down.*)

Scene 9

LIGHTS up. SCREEN shows GULICKS in theatre.

VOICE. The discovery of radioactive elements   in the late nineteenth century enabled scientists to set back the estimated age of the Earth to several billion years,   and the discovery in more recent decades   that the Universe is expanding,   this that there is a point in Time when the Universe   was tightly compressed   smaller than your tiniest fingernail!

thus that the age of the Universe is many billions of years

uncountable

Yet   humankind resides in Time,   God bless us.

Frank and Emily Gulick as we wind down *our*   time together.

What are your plans for the future?

FRANK. ... Oh that is, that's hard to   that's hard to answer.

EMILY. It depends I guess on

FRANK. Mr. Filco had advised

EMILY. I guess it's,

next is the grand jury

FRANK. Yes: the grand jury.

Mr. Filco cannot be present for the session   to protect our boy I don't understand the law, just the prosecutor is there

swaying the jurors' minds

Oh I try to understand but I can't,

EMILY. he says we should be prepared

we should be prepared for a trial

VOICE. You are ready for the trial   to clear your son's name?

FRANK. Oh yes ...

EMILY. yes that is a way of,   of putting it

Yes.   To clear Carl's name.

FRANK. ... Oh yes you have to be realistic.

EMILY. Yes but before that   the true murderer of Edith Kaminsky

might come forward.

If the true murderer is watching this   *Please come forward.*

FRANK. ... Well we both believe Carl is protecting someone, some friend   another boy

EMILY. the one who really   committed that terrible crime

FRANK. So all we can do is pray.   Pray Carl will come   to his senses   give police the other boy's name, or I believe this: if it's a friend of Carl's

he must have some decency   in his heart

VOICE. Your faith   in your son remains unshaken?

EMILY. You would have had to see his   toes,

his tiny baby toes in his bath.

His curly hair,   splashing in the bath.

His yellow rompers or no: I guess that was Denny

FRANK. If your own flesh and blood looks you in the eye,

you believe

EMILY. Oh yes.

VOICE. Human personality, it might be theorized, is a phenomenon of memory yet memory   built up from cells, and   atoms   does not "exist":   thus memory   like mind   like personality

is but a fiction?

EMILY. Oh   remembering backward is so hard!

oh it's,

FRANK. it pulls your brain in two.

EMILY. This medication the doctor gave me, my mouth   my mouth is so dry

In the middle of the night I wake up drenched in

FRANK. You don't know who you are   until a thing like this happens,

then you don't know.

EMILY. It tears your brain in two, trying to remember,

like even looking at the pictures

Oh you are lost

FRANK. in Time you are lost

EMILY. You fall and fall,

... ever since the,   the butcher shop
he wasn't always himself   but
who he was then, I don't know.
It's so hard, remembering why.
FRANK. Yes my wife means thinking backward the
way   the way the police make you, so many questions
you start forgetting right away   it comes out crazy.

Like now,   right here   I don't remember anything
up to now   I mean, I can't swear to it: the first time,
you see, we just lived. We lived in our house. I am a, I am
a post office employee   I guess I said that?   well, we
live in our,   our house.   I mean, it was the first time
through.   Just living. Like the t.v., the picture's always
on, if nobody's watching it you know?   So, the people
we were then,   I guess I'm trying to say
    those actual people me and her   the ones you see *here*
    aren't them. (*Laughs.*)
I guess that sounds crazy,
VOICE. We have here the heartbeat   of parental
love and faith, it's a beautiful thing   Frank and Molly
Gulick, please comment?
FRANK. We are that boy's father and mother.
We know that our son is not a murderer and a,   a
rapist
EMILY. We know, if that girl came to harm   there is
some reason   for it to be revealed, but
EMILY. They never found the knife, for one thing
FRANK. or whatever it was
EMILY. They never found the knife, the murderer could
tell them where it's buried, or   whatever it was.
Oh he could help us so   if he just would.
VOICE. And your plans for the future,   Mr. and Mrs.
Gulick of Lakepointe, NJ?
FRANK. ... Well.
I guess,   I guess we don't have any.

(*Long silence, to the point of awkwardness.*)

VOICE. ... Plans for the future, Mr. and Mrs. Gulick of Lakepointe, NJ?

FRANK. The thing is, you discover   you need to be protected from your own thoughts sometimes,   but who is there to do it?

EMILY. God didn't make any of us strong enough I guess.

FRANK. Look: one day in a family like this, it's like the next day   and the day before.

EMILY. You could say it *is* the next day, I mean the same   the same day.

FRANK. Until one day it isn't

(*LIGHTS out.*)

The End

COSTUME PLOT

Frank Gulick: beige polyester shirt; beige and blue stripe polyester tie; tan polyester pants; tooled belt with western buckle; dark brown polyester sportcoat (too large); off-white nylon socks; brown crepe sole shoes

Emily Gulick: navy blue Leslie Fay dress; grey mid-length cotton jacket; panty hose; grey low pumps; hairnet; silver pin and earrings; hanky

PROPERTY PLOT

Two metal cups with water. Frank's full, Emily's one-quarter full (for knock over); Emily's purse with hanky.

THE ECLIPSE
a play in eight scenes

CHARACTERS

MURIEL WASHBURN, 76 years old

STEPHANIE WASHBURN, 38 years old

AILEEN STANLEY, mid-30's

SEÑOR RíOS, mid-50's

NOTE: Though there are occasional surreal or fanciful elements in the play, its dominant tone is serious; it should never be allowed to degenerate into situation comedy. The actress playing Muriel should be particularly wary of succumbing to a stereotypical comic stance vis-a-vis the audience. To the contrary, both Muriel and Stephanie are intelligent, troubled, complex women whose employment of humor is for the sake of relief or diversion.

As the play unfolds in quick scenes, the shadow of the eclipse moves slowly but inexorably across the stage. At certain times, as indicated, it is noticed (by Muriel); most of the time it appears to have been assimilated into the unexamined routine of their lives.

Scene 1

*LIGHTS up. The Washburns' apartment, or a stylized
approximation of it. Stage right, toward rear, is
Muriel's bedroom (dimly seen): stage left, toward rear,
is Stephanie's bedroom (dimly seen); center stage, a
living area. Suggestion of old but good furniture,
somewhat heavy in design; a cluster of new brightly
colored pillows on a sofas, a well-worn Oriental carpet
on the floor; old-fashioned oak bookcases crammed with
books, both hardcover and paperback. On the wall above
the sofa there is a framed work of art that appears to be
in the style of abstract expressionism (but is really a
photograph of a planetary nebula). On a portable
wheeled table is a television set. Though the apartment
is empty the television set is turned on with its volume
high.*

*In this first scene the ECLIPSE is a sliver of darkness at
extreme stage right, scarcely noticeable as it blends with
the shadowy interior of Muriel's room.*

*Door in rear wall opens: MURIEL WASHBURN enters,
followed closely by her daughter STEPHANIE who,
though burdened with packages, is trying to assist her
even as MURIEL, offended and upset, shrinks away.*

*MURIEL is an older woman of quicksilver moods. SHE is
attractive though superficially flamboyant, hyperactive,
"busy"; her mannerisms, in imitation of nervousness,
may in fact be designed to disguise nervousness. Here is
a woman approaching old age—disintegration, death—
and alternately fascinated by and terrified of the changes
occurring in her. In this scene she is wearing a brassy
wig which is slightly askew on her head. (But only*

47

slightly: it must not be comically crooked.) She wears a raincoat with iridescent threads, a hood, deep pockets—a coat that is much too large for her, reaching almost to her ankles; SHE carries an oversized shopping bag or purse, with a gold or silver sparkle to it. Beneath the coat she is wearing what appear to be pedal pushers and a sweater. In contrast, STEPHANIE is wearing a beige tweed blazer and matching pants; a dark brown turtleneck sweater; fashionable shoes or boots; SHE carries an attractive handbag of dark brown leather, as well as an armful of grocery packages and a skirt or a dress from the dry cleaner's. STEPHANIE is a handsome woman who looks younger than her age; she is slender, but strong-bodied; SHE moves forthrightly and with confidence, a "public" person, except at such times—and this is one of those times—when SHE is frightened and angry, having lost control of a situation. Her exasperation with Muriel should not entirely obscure the fact of her intense love for the woman.

STEPHANIE. (*Close to tears, her fear expressed as anger:*) *Why* did you do that. Mother, when you promised! Why such a—deranged thing!

MURIEL. (*Facing audience, back to Stephanie: agitated but trying to appear calm.*) How dare you call me deranged! Who are you!

STEPHANIE. (*Voice raised to be heard over the television:*) Behaving like that—in that store. Now we'll have to get our groceries over at the A&P on Third Avenue. (*As SHE sets down her packages, one tips over and spills several oranges, which, distracted, SHE stoops to pick up.*) God damn it, Mother—

MURIEL. I'm Muriel.

STEPHANIE.—you promised.

MURIEL. I—I didn't want them to charge us twice.

STEPHANIE. Nobody was going to charge us twice.

MURIEL. (*As if groping:*) It's easy to be cheated in those stores. The way the check-out woman slides those things along, everything automatic ... (*With increasing anger.*) They were watching us. As soon as we came in, they started. The, what's the word, the surveillance people—I can sense it.

STEPHANIE. (*Switching off television.*) Nobody was watching you, Mother. Why would anyone watch you! (*Laughs dispiritedly.*) Behaving the way you do, so entirely unpredictable, dressed like you are, why would anyone watch you!

MURIEL. (*Clapping her hands over her ears, dislodging her wig just perceptibly.*) It's too quiet in here suddenly. It isn't natural.

STEPHANIE. (*Ironically.*) I turned off the television, Mother. Now that we're home we can make our own noises, to scare off burglars.

MURIEL. I don't like too much quiet, my head echoes.

STEPHANIE. You promised you wouldn't act—that way, you promised.

MURIEL. It wasn't "that way"—it was ... (*A pause.*) another way.

STEPHANIE. There are people who recognize me in those stores—from my picture in the newspaper, from television. I'm so ashamed. (*As the items from the dry cleaner's begin to slide to the floor, STEPHANIE snatches them up and tosses them back down onto the sofa.*) You know better, God damn it. And flirting like that with the butcher—

MURIEL. He was flirting with me. One of my students from the old days, now he's almost my age—an old man. Y'know why? Because particles speed up as they approach black holes—cross the "event horizon." (*As if warningly.*) I don't get any younger but the rest of you get older, fast.

STEPHANIE. That butcher? He was a student of yours?

MURIEL. Look, I had a long teaching career. Half the goddam city—half the goddam country—are former students of "Mrs. Washburn," Commodore Stephen Decatur Junior High School. (*Laughs.*) There's no escape!

STEPHANIE. And that ridiculous coat of yours—I'm going to throw it away. You've become a clown!

MURIEL. (*Backing off.*) Oh no you don't. (*Hugs coat tightly about her.*)

STEPHANIE. Why did you behave the way you did?

MURIEL. What way?

STEPHANIE. Why did you throw those things on the floor?

MURIEL. I didn't throw them, they fell.

STEPHANIE. Yes? Up over the side of the cart?

MURIEL. Don't you raise your voice to me, baby.

STEPHANIE. Then talking so fast. Practically punching me when I touched you.

MURIEL. (*Pained.*) I—didn't know who it was. Laying hands on me. (*Hesitates.*) These icy-cold little hands. Out of nowhere.

STEPHANIE. (*Incensed.*) Behaving like a madwoman.

MURIEL. Who are you calling a madwoman? You "theorist"!

STEPHANIE. You said you wanted to go shopping— said you were bored at home. And then—you betrayed me.

MURIEL. They're watching you too—with their electronic eyes. Don't think you can escape. (*Defiantly.*) Who said I was bored? I'm never bored. Somebody else must've said that.

STEPHANIE. —Losing control like that. In public.

MURIEL. (*Drawing in a deep breath, pausing, then shrieking.*) I DID NOT LOSE CONTROL! I DO NOT LOSE CONTROL!

(There is a long tense moment: the WOMEN stand motionless, perfectly poised. We sense how skillfully MURIEL holds Stephanie in check.)

MURIEL. *(Calmer, almost conversationally.)* I am *never* bored when alone. I am *only* bored in company.

STEPHANIE. *(Retreating, taking a package out of one of the grocery bags, murmuring to herself.)* Oh—it's leaking. All over the inside of—

MURIEL. It's just they were watching me. From the first instant I stepped through the what do you call it— *(Snaps fingers, trying to remember term.)*—the seeing-eye door.

STEPHANIE. You cracked the damn thing—the plastic container. *(Peering inside.)* "Seafood combo"—$8.25 a pound. Half of it isn't even real, it's "sea legs." Manufactured in Japan from parts of fish scraps, and dyed pink.

MURIEL. *(Earnestly.)* Not just watching—I could live with that—I was born in this century. But *taping.* On *microfilm.* Hiding up in the ceiling, the surveillance people. Putting us all on file. *(Hugs herself again in the coat: we see that the pockets are bulging.)*

STEPHANIE. If you're so afraid of people watching you—why the hell make a spectacle of yourself?

MURIEL. *(Shrewdly.)* To distract them, Stevie. It's an old, old trick of evolution: distracting predators. *(Flaps her arms, mugs, winks toward audience.)* First principle of teaching junior high school. *(MURIEL does a little tap dance, is surprisingly agile.)*

STEPHANIE. *(Close to tears, yet amused; then reverts to her reproachful tone.)* Now I can't shop at that Kroger's any more, and the A&P is a mile away. And you caused such a fuss in the Italian bakery—

MURIEL. It's all in your imagination, we could go back any time.

STEPHANIE. —and the Rexall's. (*Laughs dispiritedly.*) If this keeps up we'll have to move out of the neighborhood.

MURIEL. (*As if seriously.*) The elderly provoke the acceleration of objects in their vicinity: things *fly* into their pockets. Clocks speed up. Calendars. Pulses.

STEPHANIE. It isn't funny. How can I possibly go to Denver next month and leave you alone...

MURIEL. (*Continuing, with eerie precision.*) If—and when—the earth's density increases its volume must contract, and when its volume contracts to the size of a pea (*With thumb and forefinger raised overhead, indicates the size of a pea.*), it will implode—and become a black hole. And time will cease. And all our problems will be solved.

(*A moment's silence.*)

STEPHANIE. (*Makes an impatient gesture.*) No wonder you scared your students! (*Pause.*) When is *that* going to happen? In a million million years?

(*MURIEL shrugs.*)

STEPHANIE. You've been so—almost—sensible—for weeks, and now this. What am I going to do?

(*MURIEL has drifted off toward stage right, though not in the direction of her bedroom [at the rear]. SHE has placed her left hand over her left eye and seems to be testing the vision. As STEPHANIE, not noticing, carries one of the grocery bags into another room (presumably into the kitchen, offstage), MURIEL behaves oddly, removing her hand from her eye,*

*replacing it quizzically, testing her other eye. [It is the
"eclipse"—a shadow growing in her brain—which she
sees or senses.])*

MURIEL. My eye ... A blade of—dark.
STEPHANIE. (*Calling out to her, preoccupied.*) At
least take off that coat. Help me put the things away.
MURIEL. Or is it in both eyes? No. Yes ...
STEPHANIE. Mother? What is it?

(*MURIEL mutters to herself inaudibly. STEPHANIE
approaches.*)

STEPHANIE. Your eye? Your vision? What?
MURIEL. Nothing.
STEPHANIE. Is something wrong? (*STEPHANIE is
impeccably well groomed, but at this moment runs a hand
through her hair, disheveling it.*)—You know your eyes are
sensitive to light but you don't protect them. That bright
sun—
MURIEL. (*With a sudden harsh laugh.*) I'm all right,
mind your own business. Your own eyes.
STEPHANIE. (*Uncertainly.*) Mother, please? Is
something wrong?
MURIEL. (*Muttering as if frightened, defensive.*)
Nothing wrong with me, what's wrong with *you*? Always
spying on me—the lot of you.
STEPHANIE. Mother—
MURIEL. Who's "Mother"? I'm Muriel.
STEPHANIE. Look—if something is wrong you'd
better tell me. I'll make an appointment with Dr.
Weisbord.
MURIEL. Oh—hell. Go fly off to Denver, fly off to
Paris, or Istanbul, or Hoboken—wherever. Who needs you?
I have my own friends.

(STEPHANIE advances upon her but MURIEL wards her off.)

STEPHANIE. *(Half pleading.)* Mother—should I call Doctor. You haven't seen him since July.

MURIEL. Who's "Mother"? You're a feminist, baby, I'm a feminist. Oh boy am I a feminist—I was there when it was invented . So who's "Mother"?

STEPHANIE. Oh for God's sake, here we go again.

MURIEL *(Addressing audience.)* Who gets stuck with "Mother" gets stuck scrubbing the toilets—right?

STEPHANIE. *(Exasperated.) You* haven't scrubbed a toilet in this apartment in thirty years!

MURIEL And it looks it, too.

STEPHANIE. *Are* you all right? Just tell me.

MURIEL. *(Takes a hand mirror out of her pocket, shoves it in STEPHANIE's face in a brusque gesture.)* Look at yourself, baby, not me. You're the Ph. D. You're the professor. You pay the bills around here, not me.

STEPHANIE. *(Flinches from the sight of her own reflection, oddly; then renews her tack.)* I'd better call Dr. Weisbord.

MURIEL. *(Quickly.)* The problem is—you're ashamed of me. Of your own dear mother, ashamed. "Prominent Feminist Ashamed of Her Own Dear Mother."

STEPHANIE. I am not—ashamed. I'm worried.

MURIEL. "I'm worried!"

STEPHANIE. *(Clutching Muriel's wrist, trying to hold her still so SHE can look into Muriel's eyes.)* Don't mock me, please. It isn't you. It's—that other person.

(A pause. MURIEL disengages herself, with an air of dignity.)

STEPHANIE. The way you lost control in the store—it wasn't you was it?

MURIEL (*Defiantly.*) I told you: I didn't want those crooks to charge us twice.

STEPHANIE. God damn it, Mother—you know it's just routine, they staple the, the (*SHE becomes nervous, rattled, speaking rapidly.*) receipts to the bags—from the deli counter—you know that. (*Locates one of the bags, with a stapled receipt, to show to Muriel who airily ignores it.*) Nobody was going to make us pay twice. And even if, if—if they tried to—why throw things onto the *floor*? Like a madwoman?

MURIEL. (*Contemptuously.*) What do you—*you*!—know about madness!

(*A pause. MURIEL changes tone, reverts to her flamboyant, stagey self. From this point until the end of the scene, the LIGHTS should dim at the periphery of the action, focusing upon MURIEL and STEPHANIE, with MURIEL at the center, as if greedy for attention.*)

MURIEL. *She* who lasts, laughs. (*SHE pats one of her deep pockets, pulls out an item—a box of gourmet chocolates; professes surprise.*) Why—what have we here? (*Out of that same pocket, SHE pulls a jar of fancy cocktail shrimp.*) Uh-oh—what's this? (*Out of another pocket, a mango.*) And *this*?

(*STEPHANIE is utterly astonished, watching with wide childlike eyes. A strand of hair has fallen into her face and her posture is less assured than it was only a few minutes ago.*)

STEPHANIE. Oh my God, Mother—what have you done?

MURIEL. "Mother"? I'm Muriel.

STEPHANIE. But—when did you take those things? How? I was watching you every second.

MURIEL. (*Chuckling.*) Now you see it—voila! Now you don't! (*A small jar of caviar in the palm of her hand, then disappearing up her sleeve.*)

STEPHANIE. How could you! I trusted you!

MURIEL. Treat time for my little girl! Things you can't afford on your salary!

STEPHANIE (*Growing angry.*) I'll have to take those things back to the store.

MURIEL. What?

STEPHANIE. Back to the store. Right now. (*Half sobbing.*) Oh—I should have known better—God damn it I should have known.

MURIEL. Oh no you're not, baby. These're *mine.*

(*MURIEL tosses the mango to STEPHANIE, who has no choice but to catch it. SHE laughs, rather shrilly.*)

STEPHANIE. (*Sadly.*) It's all a joke to you now, isn't it?

MURIEL. What's a joke? (*Sniffs under an arm.*) Where?

STEPHANIE. Life. (*Speaking slowly, not quite accusingly.*) The life remaining to you.

MURIEL. Nah—I'm imbued with the ""tragic sense of life," you betcha. Teach in any American public school for forty years, it's natural.

STEPHANIE. Now I have to take these things back. These—God—damned—things. (*Quietly furious. It is evident that STEPHANIE is deflecting her deep concern for Muriel's health along lines of a more conventional emotional exasperation, disgust. SHE picks up the items flamboyantly, wiping tears from her eyes.*) God *damn*, and *damn*, and *damn*.

MURIEL. Aw Stevie where's your sense of humor? (*Snatches one of the items from her, drops it in her pocket.*)

STEPHANIE. Give that back! Mother—damn *you!*

MURIEL. (*Less certainly.*) Hey—Stevie?

STEPHANIE. Don't call me that ridiculous name, I hate it!

MURIEL. Don't yell at me, baby. (*As STEPHANIE snatches at one of the items.*) These things're *mine*. LOOT.

(*A brief ineffectual scuffle. STEPHANIE, though furious, sobbing in frustration, is timid about using force against her mother. When a jar falls to the floor SHE gives a little scream and kicks it offstage.*
By this time only the two women are fully illuminated.)

MURIEL. (*Hands over ears, repentant; perhaps genuinely frightened.*) Baby—why are you crying? I, I won't do it again—I promise. (*Pause.*) I won't go shopping with you again.

STEPHANIE. (*Wiping face, calmer.*) That's why I'm crying, Mother—you won't go shopping with me again. Today was the last time.

(*LIGHTS darken. WOMEN stand motionless. As LIGHTS go out:*)

MURIEL. (*With bravado.*) Who's "Mother"? I'm Muriel.

(*LIGHTS out.*)

Scene 2

LIGHTS up. It is several days later, in the evening. MURIEL in an attractive quilted bathrobe, a colorful turban wrapped around her head, sits on the sofa composing a letter on numerous sheets of pink stationery. A vase of slightly (not overly) wilted gladioli, flame-colored, is on the coffee table and MURIEL glances up frequently at it as if for inspiration.

The "blade of dark" is slightly more prominent now, stage right, cutting through Muriel's bedroom at the rear.

In the doorway of her own bedroom, observing her mother closely and out of the range of Muriel's vision, STEPHANIE stands talking in an apparently surreptitious way on the telephone. In this scene both women speak clearly enough to be heard by the audience and yet not by each other. STEPHANIE has recovered from her upset of the previous day and is again impeccably groomed, in tweed trousers, turtleneck sweater, medallion necklace around her throat. As SHE speaks, her eyes drift about in the characteristic manner of one talking on the telephone, yet always return to Muriel. Unconsciously STEPHANIE winds the telephone cord around her fingers, wrist, etc.)

STEPHANIE. Except for last Thursday, she's been fine. Even docile. (*Laughs.*) For *her.*

MURIEL. (*Writing her letter, cheerily.*) Señor Ríos, thank you so much for the LOVELY flowers.

STEPHANIE. The reason I'm calling, Jill, is—well, you know I've been nominated for executive director of the Council, I need to be there, and I thought maybe, I'd hoped—(*In a rush.*)—you could come stay with Mother for a few days?

MURIEL. How did you know (*Peering at gladioli.*) flame-colored glads, fluorescent-bright glads, are my favorite flowers?

STEPHANIE. No, she isn't listening in on the extension, Jill. I can *see* her.

MURIEL. I wish I could speak Spanish to express my sentiments more lyrically ...

STEPHANIE. (*Watching Muriel.*) I was never Mother's favorite, really. She loved us equally. I mean—loves. She asks after you all the time. And David, and Betsey. And Jenny. *Yes.*

MURIEL. (*Alternately girlish and seductive.*) Of course, there *is* a minor age discrepancy. For forty-two years I taught ... (*Hesitates; rethinks.*) ... no, dummy, strike that: for a *number* of years I taught junior high school science.

STEPHANIE. Jill, I can't. She refuses to allow any nurse in this apartment since ... you know. And it *is* her apartment really ... in spirit ... though I pay the rent. (*Listens; nods; frowns impatiently.*)

MURIEL. Señor Ríos, you make me shy. The other day in the park....

STEPHANIE. Yes yes right. Yes but *no.* A nursing home is absolutely out of the question for the present. Not until it's ... inescapable. You saw what happened when she was in the hospital: begging everybody to be allowed to die.

MURIEL. I've been a widow for so long ... (*Pause, rethinks.*) Naw! What if he finds out the truth! (*Crumples letter, tosses down; takes up another sheet of stationery.*)

STEPHANIE. (*Urgent.*) Would you like to talk to her? She *does.* Oh she *does.* Jill, please, we aren't small children anymore, we aren't *rivals.* Women must stop perceiving themselves as *rivals.* We're *sisters.*

MURIEL. (*Musing.*) Perhaps you don't believe in divorce in your native country, Señor Ríos ... but my husband and I parted ... divorced ... in 1957. Oh he was a cruel cold-hearted son of a—(*Pauses.*) Oh he meant well, he was just ineffectual, sort of *not there.*

STEPHANIE. (*Intense.*) Only for a week, Jill. I simply must attend this conference. No there isn't "internal disagreement," that's just the media. The issue is—some of us believe it's time for women to form a third political party.

MURIEL. (*Continuing with a flourish.*) But when genuine love, old-fashioned romance, is involved ... I am, you'll discover, practically a girl again; a *virgin.*

STEPHANIE. Oh, she's writing a letter. This latest "friend"—"man friend."

MURIEL. I hope to be swept away.

STEPHANIE. Of course it's a delusion—what else? (*Nervous laugh.*) He even sends her flowers....

MURIEL. Huh?

STEPHANIE. arranged by Mother herself ...

MURIEL. What's this?

STEPHANIE. Or, I guess retrieved out of the garbage dumpster—which is what these look like.

(*MURIEL's mood suddenly changes; we see that SHE is susceptible to swift emotional swings as if, indeed, another person entered her being. SHE clumsily tries to hide the letter SHE has been writing, muttering to herself, "Can't let—Evidence used against me—Spies— Surveillance—" but these words need not be clearly articulated. STEPHANIE sees that MURIEL is upset, but it is too late.*)

MURIEL. (*Furious, as vase of gladioli capsizes.*)
LOOK WHAT YOU MADE ME DO! Clumsy clumsy—
idiot! Spying on your own flesh-and-blood!

(*As MURIEL tries awkwardly to gather up the gladioli,
STEPHANIE hastily concludes her conversation.*)

STEPHANIE. (*In an undertone.*) Oh God. I have to
hang up—Will you think about it please? Good-bye.

(*When STEPHANIE hurries to help MURIEL—who
appears to have banged her knee on the coffee table as
well—MURIEL slaps at her.*)

MURIEL. I caught you! Red-handed! Spying on me! In
my own house!
STEPHANIE. Oh Mother, I—
MURIEL. Who were you talking to?—Reporting to?
STEPHANIE. (*Placatingly, guiltily.*) I was talking to
a—
MURIEL. Don't lie: it was the school board, wasn't it?
STEPHANIE. The school board?
MURIEL. Those fools!—Is that who it was? Checking
up on me? And my own daughter cooperating?
STEPHANIE. Oh no—no. It wasn't the school board,
Mother. It was—a colleague of mine. (*STEPHANIE
replaces the gladioli in the vase, dabs up some of the water
spilled on the coffee table, carries the vase offstage as if to
replenish the water: continues speaking, trying to calm
Muriel.*)—a colleague of *mine.* A—
MURIEL. ... Spying on me. And I am helpless. (*SHE
presses her left hand against her left eye, a pained
expression on her face.*) Paralyzed under the ... anesthetic.

(*STEPHANIE returns with the flowers in the vase, sets the vase down. But MURIEL is too upset to be placated.*)

STEPHANIE.(*With forced sincerity.*) It was ... a friend. A woman from the Council.

MURIEL. Whosit?

STEPHANIE. The Council. The Feminist Majority Council. Where I'm running for office—

MURIEL. So why are they spying on me? I'm not running for office. (*Laughs angrily.*)

STEPHANIE. Nobody was spying on you.

MURIEL. *You* were: I saw you.

STEPHANIE. For God's sake, Mother. I was just standing there. I have to stand somewhere.

MURIEL. You're saying the apartment is too small? I should leave? Is that it? You're hinting I should leave?

STEPHANIE. What? Of course not.

MURIEL. (*With bravado.*) I can leave, just like that. (*Snaps fingers.*) I've had ... invitations. To be a house guest. I've had a proposal ... to elope.

STEPHANIE. Don't be silly, it's your apartment.

MURIEL. It used to be, now it's yours. Too small for two career women. Matter and anti-matter. Protons. Trouble. *You* own it now, you can do as you please. (*Breathing hard, incensed.*) All I need is enough boxes.

STEPHANIE. Enough what?

MURIEL. Boxes.

STEPHANIE. What about boxes?

MURIEL.To pack my things.

STEPHANIE (*Laughing.*) Oh Mother, really—

MURIEL. Who's "Mother"? I'm—

STEPHANIE. Muriel.

MURIEL. *I'm* Muriel.

(STEPHANIE notices the sheets of stationery MURIEL has tried to hide under one of the pillows but makes it a point to ignore them. Instead, SHE arranges the pillows in order to conceal them more. MURIEL rubs rather dazedly at her eyes.)

STEPHANIE. It's late, we should both get to bed.

MURIEL. You think I'm deluded, don't you?

STEPHANIE. What?

MURIEL. You *thought* it—could hear you.

STEPHANIE. I—did not think it.

MURIEL. Baby, Muriel Washburn has worn out more "delusions" than most other people have worn out Kleenex in their lifetimes. So don't tell me about "delusions."

STEPHANIE. Oh—Mother. You make too much of things.

MURIEL. It's possible to read thoughts, if you know how. Microwave radiation. Permeating the universe. It was only discovered in 1964 but I could sense it all my life ...

STEPHANIE. I'm sorry I upset you. Why don't you ...

MURIEL. *(Earnestly.)* It *was* the school board, wasn't it? The superintendent's office?

STEPHANIE. No Mother. All that was—a long time ago.

MURIEL. Those liars. Calling me "hysterical." They wouldn't believe how I was followed, and that ... that bloody chicken foot in my desk. *(A shiver of disgust.)* They wouldn't take me seriously until I was murdered. In my own classroom.

STEPHANIE. Yes but you're all right now. You're fine now. You're retired.

MURIEL. A twelve-year-old with a razor. They wouldn't believe me.

STEPHANIE. You're retired now, the hell with them. Why don't I run a bath for you—

MURIEL. It *was* the school board, wasn't it? Just tell the truth.

STEPHANIE. I—I am telling the truth. It was a friend of mine.

MURIEL. (*Regarding her closely, searchingly.*) And you weren't talking about me behind my back?

STEPHANIE. Of course not, Mother.

MURIEL. (*Seems about to believe Stephanie; then changes her tone.*) Nah—I don't believe you. There's proof.

STEPHANIE. Proof?

MURIEL. The glad—, glad— (*SHE is pointing to the gladioli, having difficulty pronouncing the word.*) glad-a-lols—

STEPHANIE. (*Mispronounces the word too, stammering.*) Glad—Glad-e-o-lee—

MURIEL. Glad-e-o-lee—Oh shit: these things, these—flowers. They're ruined now.

STEPHANIE. Oh no—they're fine. They're beautiful.

MURIEL. Nah—they're ruined. All withered.

STEPHANIE. Oh I think they're beautiful.

MURIEL. My friend sent them to me, he's a gentleman but shy. Dances the tango. But shy.

STEPHANIE. Senor—César?

MURIEL. Ríos. Señor Ríos.

(*LIGHT begins to fade; centers upon MURIEL who executes a few dance steps, vaguely resembling the tango. Brief rise of tango MUSIC, then fading.*)

MURIEL. All I need is a box. (*Pause.*) Boxes.

(*LIGHTS out.*)

STEPHANIE'S VOICE. (*Shrilly.*) Oh Mother—you make too much of things!

Scene 3

*LIGHTS up, but only to focus upon MURIEL who stands,
in her quilted bathrobe and turban, center stage.*

MURIEL. (*Reciting, in a girl's bell-like voice.*)
I saw Eternity the other night,
Like a great ring of pure and endless light ...

*(In silence, MURIEL removes her turban: exposes her bare
head. SHE has had neurosurgery, and her gunmetal-gray
hair is cropped short. At the left side of her head and
across the crown there is a patch of fuzz beneath which
a jagged scar of nine or ten inches in length is
prominent.*
*MURIEL stands with her head bowed, turban unwound in
her fingers, as the LIGHTS fade.)*

Scene 4

*LIGHTS up. A lively, boisterous episode, in contrast with
the preceding. Here is MURIEL in one of her
hyperkinetc moods watching a boxing match (Tyson-
Biggs) on television. SHE is wearing crimson stretch
pants, a velour shirt, jogging shoes, and the brassy wig
of Scene 1. Her color is good, her eyes bright. SHE
stands in front of the set mimicking certain of the
boxers' movements—feinting, jabbing, throwing
punches, footwork, "slipping" punches by turning her
head swiftly. The television screen is not seen by the*

*audience but there are CROWD NOISES, an
ANNOUNCER'S VOICE, the sound of of an
occasional BELL. MURIEL, caught up in the action,
mutters "C'mon!" "Yeah—like that!" "Deck 'im!"
"Don't let 'im get away!" "C'mon Mike—ice 'im!" etc.*
STEPHANIE *is visible in her bedroom, pacing about,
papers in hand, practicing a speech; SHE pauses to
contemplate herself in a mirror. Very shortly, however,
the noise from the living room distracts her and brings
her out. [See Appendix at rear of play for Stephanie's
speech.]*
*By this time the "eclipse" covers about two-fifths of the
stage, from stage right. Muriel's bedroom is dark.*

STEPHANIE. (*Approaching the set, staring in
revulsion.*) What are you watching?—Oh, Mother! My
God! *Box*ing?

(*MURIEL continues with her feinting, jabbing,etc.*)

STEPHANIE. You're watching a *box*ing match?
MURIEL. (*Waves her off.*) Don't distract me—go
away.
STEPHANIE. Mother, Are you serious? When have
you gotten interested in—
MURIEL. Shhhh! It's Mike Tyson! (*Cringing, excited.*)
Oh wow, what a left hook!
STEPHANIE. (*Fascinated, disgusted.*) Which one is
Mike Tyson?
MURIEL. If you have to ask, you can't be told. (*Stands
stock-still, whistling thinly through her teeth as the BELL
rings signaling the end of a round.*
STEPHANIE. (*Switches the set off primly.*) You can't
be serious. You're just—
MURIEL. (*Offended.*) Hey—whadja *do*? What the hell?

STEPHANIE. —just pretending.

MURIEL. I don't interfere with *your* cultural interests.

STEPHANIE. I couldn't hear myself think, with this on so loud. It sounded like the monkey house at the zoo.

(*MURIEL switches the set back on; STEPHANIE switches it off again.*)

STEPHANIE. You know you shouldn't get excited. Worked up. (*With a despairing laugh.*) I can't *believe* this.

MURIEL. (*Flippantly.*) Seein's believin'! (*SHE switches the set back on, prevents Stephanie from switching it off. Her face registers intense empathetic interest.*)

STEPHANIE. Which one did you say is Mike Tyson?

MURIEL. The little one.

STEPHANIE. *That* one?

(*The BELL rings again, signaling the start of the next round. MURIEL resumes her crouch and her comical movements; STEPHANIE watches with disdain.*)

MURIEL. C'mon! Like that! Ummmmm—what a left hook! Didja see that left hook!

STEPHANIE. Is that *real*?

MURIEL. Huh?

STEPHANIE. Is that *real*?—*real blood*? On that poor man's face?

MURIEL. Oh wow! (*Wincing.*)

STEPHANIE. Mother—you *are* crazy. I can't *believe* this.

(*MURIEL pushes her vaguely to one side, but STEPHANIE manages to switch off the set again.*)

MURIEL. Why can't I watch?

STEPHANIE. It excites you too much, that's why not. (*Passes a hand over her face.*) My God—it's horrible. Why anyone in her right mind would want to see it I can't imagine.

MURIEL. (*Cheerfully, insolently.*) Yah so what—it's only a replay. I saw it already, I know how Mike winds it up. (*Throws a zippy left hook.*) Vintage Tyson 1989.

STEPHANIE. You've seen it already? That fight? You were watching it for the second time?

MURIEL. (*Mopping her face with her shirt.*) Muriel does lots of things, sweetie, nights you're out campaigning.

STEPHANIE. (*Stung.*) Mother, I do not "campaign."

MURIEL. "Networking," then.

STEPHANIE. I do not "network." I—

MURIEL. Old-fashioned politicking, then. Whatever.

STEPHANIE. You do this sort of thing to upset me, don't you. It's a pattern.

MURIEL. (*Laying a heavy hand on Stephanie's shoulder.*) Oh—pfffff! Your father always made that accusation. "You do it to upset me, don't you! Me, me, me!" (*Shakes head.*) Some people imagine the universe revolves around their precious navels.

STEPHANIE. (*Calmly.*) You know this is a crucial period in my career. I've been working for the Council for years and I—I deserve some national recognition. On Sunday, when I leave, I won't know if—if I can trust you here. If—I can trust you.

MURIEL. (*Airily.*) That's for me to know and you to find out. (*Placing a hand over one of her eyes, quizzically, though not concerned or upset.*) One of these light bulbs is burned out, I guess. (*SHE sits on the sofa, leans back to peer up inside the shade of a floor lamp, turns the switch experimentally. It is a lamp with three light bulbs of varying watts.*) Why's it so dark in here...?

STEPHANIE. (*Pacing about, takes no notice. SHE runs her hands through her hair, disturbing it smoothness.*) It's a pattern, isn't it. I begin to see. To see clearly. (*As if presenting a classroom analysis, brisk, grim, satisfied.*) You, Mother, are of that generation of women who "sacrificed" for their daughters; who wanted us to "go beyond" you. And now that we have, now you resent us. You boast about us to your friends—or did—but, secretly, you resent us.

MURIEL. (*Fussing with the lamp.*) Oh—damn!

STEPHANIE. Just when I need your support, need to trust you, you—start behaving—(*A pause.*)—like that. Like (*Another pause.*) that other person.

MURIEL. (*A strange bodiless cry.*) I don't know who it is.

(*A moment's tension: then STEPHANIE consciously breaks the spell, moving briskly about, pushing the portable television off to one side; tidying up.*)

STEPHANIE. My father—Dwight James Washburn— who *was* he? Why is he such a mystery? You've never even shown Jill and me pictures of him.

MURIEL. (*Resuming her earlier mood.*) He didn't photograph.

STEPHANIE. What?

MURIEL. Some people aren't photogenic, your father wasn't photographic. He didn't *develop*.

STEPHANIE. You make a joke of everything. The fact is—you erased half of our heritage. Jill and me. No wonder she married the first man who asked her—

MURIEL. —And you ran from the first man who asked *you.*

STEPHANIE. Men don't "ask" women to marry them, these days. You're behind the time. It's—different.

MURIEL. Whatever he asked you, you sure ran.

STEPHANIE. (*Irritably.*) There wasn't a "he," I mean—there were several. I mean (*Stammering.*)—t-there were friends, colleagues who were men, but—but it didn't work out.

MURIEL. (*Stretching.*) *That* was quite a work-out—I'm famished! Time for midnight snack!

STEPHANIE. (*A mild gesture of revulsion.*) Not me, thank you.

(*MURIEL bounces up from the sofa and trots into the kitchen. STEPHANIE is aware of the darkness on one side of the living room, but only casually turns on a small table lamp extreme stage right.*)

STEPHANIE. (*In an ordinary voice, as if addressing invisible audience.*) It was unjust to Jill and me, depriving us of a father.

MURIEL. (*Though still offstage, cheerily.*) SO SUE ME!

(*STEPHANIE presses her fingertips against her eyes in a gesture reminiscent of Muriel.*)

MURIEL. (*Returning with two cans of beer, a quart container of ice cream, two spoons.*) Working out in the ring, you get *famished.* C'mon, baby. (*Sits luxuriantly on the sofa, but Stephanie refuses to join her.*)

STEPHANIE. Is he—alive? Our father?

MURIEL. (*Shrugs.*) "Our" father?—Who he?

STEPHANIE. "Dwight James Washburn."

MURIEL. (*Singing to her own tune.*)
My sweetheart's the man in the moon,

I'm gonna be meeting him soon ...

STEPHANIE. What did he look like, at least? Do I—resemble him?

MURIEL. (*Offers a beer to STEPHANIE, who politely declines; opens the other for herself.*) I was born in 1914. The year the Imperial German Army rose up. Entropy on the march! Through Brussels to France! (*Shudders, excited.*) There's been a hot time globally, ever since.

STEPHANIE. I was four years old when he—disappeared. But I can't remember him.

(*MURIEL spoons ice cream into her mouth in a slow sensuous manner; offers some to STEPHANIE, who politely declines.*)

MURIEL. I'm approaching a watershed—

STEPHANIE. What?

MURIEL. I like French Vanilla Bean Candy Almond *almost* as much as Dutch Chocolate Mint Raspberry. Yum! Try some!

STEPHANIE. (*Declining the proffered spoon.*) I try to summon back a face—but I can't. But—(*Angry laugh.*)—the person I'm talking to, in my lectures, in my books—even my speech to the Women's Council—it's *him*.

MURIEL. (*Sharply.*) The hell with that, baby. "Dwight James Washburn" *evaporated*. On a gusty autumn night in 1957. When you were four, and Jill was three—months short of being born. And where he went, the s.o.b. soon forgot to maintain child support.

STEPHANIE. You drove him out, though.

MURIEL. Who says? (*Spooning ice cream.*)

STEPHANIE. You. You used to boast. When Jill and I were children.

MURIEL. (*Shrugging.*) Now Señor Ríos ... he's different.

STEPHANIE. Who?

MURIEL. (*Quietly.*) Señor Ríos. My friend.

STEPHANIE. (*With an impatient gesture, rolling her eyes.*) Oh. Him.

MURIEL. Completely different from your basic American man. He's Spanish ... from an ancient family.

STEPHANIE. I thought he was Hispanic. From Puerto Rico.

MURIEL. (*Adamantly.*) *Span*ish. The real thing. From Castellón de las Plana.

STEPHANIE. From where?

MURIEL. (*Rolling the syllables on her tongue.*) Castellón de la Plana. The Ríos are an old noble family. Medieval. (*SHE shivers, hugs herself.*) He's so ... romantic. Not like your Anglo men, all anemic, cold-fish types. He's warm ... warm-blooded ... *dark.* His eyes are like gems, shiny and dark ... but the whites so *white.* And his teeth ... so white. (*Pause.*) I'm undecided about the moustache.

STEPHANIE. (*Skeptically.*) And you met this Señor Ríos in the park? In May? The night of the—eclipse, was it?

MURIEL. (*Seems confused for a moment.*) No I met Señor Ríos, that's to say *he* met *me,* introduced himself to *me,* the night there were shooting stars. *You* weren't there.

STEPHANIE. Where was I, then?

MURIEL. They were streaking across the sky ... the northeast ... one or two a minute. Even with the air pollution, they were beautiful. Incandescent.

STEPHANIE. There aren't shooting stars, really. That's just a—fairy tale.

MURIEL. (*Annoyed.*) So? So they're meteors? They're real enough.

STEPHANIE. "Meteors?"

MURIEL. A shower of 'em all afire. Thrown off from a comet. (*Dreamily.*) A comet's a wild, beautiful thing but the fact of it is, it's *precise*. It won't let you down.

STEPHANIE. (*A little cruelly.*) Was that the night, last May, I came home and found you on the sofa here, you woke up and didn't know where you were?—Chattering non-stop about shooting stars, like the stars could care about *you*. But no mention, then, of "Señor Ríos."

MURIEL. (*Hurt, angry.*) So—the stars don't care about us, we can care about *them*. They got the beauty, we got the brains.

STEPHANIE. So that's how Señor Ríos entered your life.

MURIEL. No need to be jealous, it's strictly platonic. Thus far.

STEPHANIE. He calls you, when I'm not home? Sends you flowers.

MURIEL. We have a date to go dancing—when you're in Denver.

STEPHANIE. Do you!

MURIEL. No need to be jealous.

STEPHANIE. (*Stung.*) Of course not, Mother. *N o* need.

MURIEL. (*In her bright insouciant way.*) Who's "Mother"? I'm—whosit. (*Sipping beer and eating ice cream contentedly.*) Y'know why I like boxing? Why I'm a fan of Mike Tyson?

STEPHANIE. (*After a perceptible pause, yet with an almost innocent cruelty.*) Because it's about brain damage—other peoples'.

(*A long awkward pause. We see that MURIEL has been wounded only by the way her spoon freezes in mid-air. But MURIEL shrugs the remark aside.*)

MURIEL. (*Brightly.*) Yah: why I like Mike Tyson, it's not what you're thinking, probably, 'cause I'm lily-white watching black men beat up on their brothers for money, no and it's not 'cause I'm thirsty for blood, or bored, or sadistic, or—any of that. Nah, I like Mike Tyson for just one thing: When he's good, there's nobody better. He knows how to get the job done!

STEPHANIE. Better go to bed now, Mother. It's late, and you over-excited yourself.

MURIEL. (*Chuckling, almost coarsely.*) Yah: *he knows how to get the job done.* The rest of 'em ... cold fish.

STEPHANIE. (*Standing over Muriel.*) You'll have to take your medication tonight.

MURIEL. I already did.

STEPHANIE. You did *not.*

MURIEL. I say I *did.*

STEPHANIE. I can't endure another night like the last time you were—over-excited.

MURIEL. You take the pills, then. (*Laughs.*) You got the problem, you take the pills.

STEPHANIE. Now Mother.

MURIEL. (*Suddenly scrambles to her feet, backs off: has dropped her beer, the ice cream container, the spoon: a quicksilver change of mood.*) I'm not "Mother"!—don't blame me!

STEPHANIE. Mother, please—don't.

MURIEL. I don't know where she is, she's—gone. *Don't blame me.*

(*STEPHANIE hides her face in her hands, as the LIGHTS darken.*
LIGHTS out then up: STEPHANIE in a chair, later that night.)

STEPHANIE. (*In a pure, bell-like voice, to herself.*)
Though I walk through the Valley of the Shadow of Death,
I will fear no evil: for thou art with me: thy rod and thy
staff they comfort me. Thous preparest a table before me in
the presence of mine enemies ...

(*LIGHTS out.*)

Scene 5

*LIGHTS up. A few days later. Baroque harpsichord MUSIC
is playing (a record or CD of Stephanie's); the mood is
subdued.*

*By now the eclipse is at the halfway point: stage right is
dark, or would be if no lamps were on; stage left is
illuminated normally. Muriel's bedroom would be
entirely dark except that SHE has turned on a bedside
crook-necked lamp with a small, intense bulb. In her
quilted bathrobe, a towel wrapped loosely around her
head, MURIEL sits up in bed feverishly writing a letter.
Her door is shut.*

*STEPHANIE, in tailored slacks and a striking cableknit
sweater, stands in the doorway of her bedroom, talking
on the telephone. Her room is brightly lit; we see an
opened suitcase on a chair, clothes laid across her bed.*

*As SHE talks on the telephone, STEPHANIE repeatedly
glances in the direction of Muriel's room; MURIEL,
intent upon her letter, does not glance around.*

STEPHANIE. (*In a good mood.*) ... No, no, everything
is fine, Barbara. I finished the speech, I think it will be
effective, and I've conferred with ... yes, right. I've been at
the University all day, on the phone. Sally Mack, she's

head of the Women's Studies Program at Berkeley, she's going to introduce me ... (*Listens, nodding.*) Yes, Mother is fine. She is.

(*From out of the relative shadows stage right, AILEEN STANLEY appears, walking slowly, as if cautiously. SHE is a solid-bodied woman with glasses, a close-cropped practical haircut, a habit of squinting frequently and brushing at her nose; SHE wears nondescript clothes, perhaps a pants suit, and carries a handbag and a well-worn briefcase. SHE shifts between uneasiness and professional arrogance, as of a naturally shy person invested with a measure of bureaucratic authority.*)

STEPHANIE. (*A bit impatient, but confident.*) Of course I won't let any of you down. I'll be there. If we are ever to establish a viable third party, a true women's party, a majority party, this is the time. This is an exciting time! The abortion issue alone ...

(*AILEEN STANLEY rings the front door (or simulates ringing the front door) of the apartment; STEPHANIE murmurs "Oh—excuse me, someone's at the door," hangs up the phone, hurries to answer the door. MURIEL, still absorbed in her letter writing, takes no notice. The harpsichord MUSIC continues in the background.*)

STEPHANIE. (*With a polite smile.*) Yes? Hello?
AILEEN. (*Blinking at Stephanie, whom SHE apparently recognizes: SHE is startled, confused, and embarrassed.*) Oh—! Hello ...
STEPHANIE. Yes?
AILEEN. (*Consults a piece of paper, as if to disguise her awkwardness.*) I ... I've come to see ... Is this the

residence of Muriel Washburn? "Retired schoolteacher"? (*Squints at the paper.*) "Thwarted astrophysicist"?

STEPHANIE. (*Perplexed.*) Well—Muriel Washburn is my mother. We share this apartment.

AILEEN. (*Blinking, smiling nervously, almost at a loss for words.*) I guess ... it *is* you? I thought maybe, the name ... I mean, I was wondering ... unless it was a coincidence ... You don't remember but we met once, a few years ago, at a women's conference in Boston. (*Laughs nervously.*) You *are* ... Stephanie Washburn of course?

STEPHANIE. (*Trying to remain cordial.*) Yes I am, but ... what do you want?

(*AILEEN quickly thrusts out her hand. STEPHANIE has no choice but to shake it.*)

AILEEN. My name is Aileen Stanley and I'm a social worker for the county but, oh!—You wouldn't remember me. I wouldn't expect you to remember me.

STEPHANIE. ... You wanted to see my ... mother?

AILEEN. (*Easing inside the door, fluttery, nervous, yet a bit aggressive. Laughs nervously.*) I can't claim to have read your book ... but I've read essays ... like, I guess, on gender? Role-playing in the professions? The misuse of power?

STEPHANIE. (*Perplexed, a bit annoyed.*) But it's ... Mother you want to see? Muriel Washburn?

AILEEN. (*Having eased into the living room, glancing quickly about, both abashed and frankly inquisitive.*) Oh isn't this attractive! So many books! Such nice music! One of these good old apartments with high ceilings and good hardwood floors ... so different from what I usually see. (*A pause.*) May I speak with your mother, Stephanie? Is she here?

STEPHANIE. Is she expecting you?

AILEEN. I think so, yes.

STEPHANIE. (*Mildly incredulous.*) *Yes?*

AILEEN. (*Quickly.*) Oh it's ... routine. I mean, there is probably some ... misunderstanding. (*Speaking rapidly, embarrassed.*) ... I'm from the County Hot-Line Crisis Center for Senior Citizens, and ...

STEPHANIE. The county what?

AILEEN. Your mother *is* here?

STEPHANIE. She's asleep. She's under medication.

(*MURIEL now looks up, alert. SHE lays aside her letter, comes to the door of her room, listens.*)

AILEEN. —May I see her ... anyway?

STEPHANIE. (*Stiffly.*) What do you mean? If Mother is asleep you can't see her—Miss Stanley.

(*STEPHANIE, beginning to be agitated, goes to switch off the harpsichord music. MURIEL opens the door of her room a crack, peers out.*)

AILEEN. Oh—"Aileen"! Please call me—

STEPHANIE. If you want to see my mother, Aileen, I suggest you come back another time. Tomorrow? Monday? Mother is at her most coherent in the mornings.

AILEEN. "Most coherent"?

STEPHANIE. Please—what do you want?

AILEEN. I ... I've told you. I want to speak with Muriel Washburn. (*Awkwardly, yet aggressively; opening briefcase and removing papers.*) I think you had better ... comply, Stephanie, with our ... office.

(*At this point, we see that MURIEL has opened the door of her room a crack, is peering out.*)

STEPHANIE. (*Her own authority now evoked.*) Are you threatening me?

AILEEN. If I don't see Mrs. Washburn and determine her ... condition. I'm afraid I will have to return with a ... warrant; and a ... police officer.

(*MURIEL has withdrawn and shuts the door; hurriedly puts on a wig, changes her robe for a good, but not overly dressy, dress; hastily applies makeup before mirror. Her wig is silvery-white, stylish and dignified; appropriate for a woman of her age. Before the mirror, SHE mutters to herself, chiding, upset, not fully audible: Oh now! Now what! Such fuss! Why don't they let us alone! Spying on us! etc.*)

STEPHANIE. (*Astonished.*) A ... police officer?

AILEEN. (*Indicating the documents.*) Your mother filed a ... complaint against you. With our office.

STEPHANIE. (*Groping backward; sitting on arm of sofa.*) I can't believe this.

AILEEN. Yes indeed she telephoned in, left a message with one of our staff—

STEPHANIE. (*With a little cry.*) Oh God! I can't believe this!

AILEEN. She sounded sort of ... emotionally distressed. Said she'd been—locked in her room? In the dark? Tied in her bed? (*Peers at document.*) "Refused a view of the sky"—?

STEPHANIE. (*Faint wail edged with anger.*) Mother! How could you!

AILEEN. (*Reading.*): "Mental cruelty ... force-feeding of narcotics ... physical and mental coercion ... mistrust ... spiritual deprivation." (*Laughs nervously.*) Of course not all of these charges could stand up in court.

STEPHANIE. (*As if dazed.*) Mother isn't well. She hasn't been well for ... a while. (*STEPHANIE begins to stand, sinks back on sofa as if light-headed. Where at the start of the scene SHE was in control, now SHE appears almost childlike, helpless. Running her fingers unconsciously through her hair.*)

AILEEN. (*Sympathetic even while still "official."*) Even if it's a false alarm, Stephanie, I have to see her. It's—the law.

(*STEPHANIE hides her face in her hands.
MURIEL throws open her door to make a dramatic entrance. Emerging into the light SHE appears quite striking in her elegant wig, attractive dress, flattering makeup. Unfortunately SHE is bare-legged and has forgotten her shoes.*)

MURIEL. (*Imperial tone.*) What on earth is this? All this commotion?
AILEEN. (*A bit intimidated.*) You are ... Muriel Washburn?
MURIEL. (*Loftily.*) And who, may I inquire, are *you*?
AILEEN. I am Aileen Stanley of the Meridian County Hot-Line Crisis Center, Senior Citizen Division. (*Extends her hand as if for a handshake, but the gesture is ignored.*) I believe you called us yesterday, Mrs. Washburn?
MURIEL. (*Coolly.*) Stephanie, who is this person? One of your campaigners?

(*STEPHANIE looks away hurt; offended.*)

AILEEN. Mrs. Washburn, I—
MURIEL. Ms.

AILEEN. —Ms. Washburn, you did telephone us, didn't you? Our emergency hot-line number? (*Checks document.*) Friday—October 6—3:50 P.M.?

MURIEL. (*Approaches Stephanie cautiously; a bit guiltily.*) Stephanie—?

(*STEPHANIE, rather like a stubborn child, shrugs; looks away.*)

MURIEL. (*To Aileen quickly.*) Look here, Ms.— Stanley? I don't know who you are or what your true business is but I will not allow false accusations to be made against my daughter, or me. (*Indignant.*) We will not be spied on, do you hear?

AILEEN. You telephoned the Crisis Center, didn't you?—To report being *abused*?

MURIEL. (*Cupping hand to ear, haughtily.*) Report *who*?

AILEEN. (*Reading.*) "Systematic and repeated abuse."

MURIEL. Hugh? Hugh *who*?

AILEEN. "Abuse."

MURIEL. (*To Stephanie.*) Hear this! It's one of our neighbors, complaining about us. Somebody named "Hugh"?

AILEEN. (*Half shouting.*) "Abuse."

MURIEL. (*Offended.*) You needn't shout young lady. No one here is deaf.

AILEEN. Mrs. Washburn, I'm here to help you if you need help. May I speak with you in private?

MURIEL. Where did you say you're from? (*Suspicious.*) The school board? You want to revoke my pension after forty-two years?

AILEEN. No, I'm from the County Crisis Center. The Senior Citizens Program. I'm here to investigate your complaint of—abuse.

MURIEL. (*Haughtily, indicating her dress.*) Do I look like a person with a complaint? I am— (*Groping.*)—an object of gentrification.

AILEEN. Oh, that is a pretty dress, Mrs. Washburn. You look very nice. But according to our records —

MURIEL. Do I look like a senior citizen? (*Winking toward audience.*) I may be "senior," but I sure ain't a "citizen."

AILEEN. (*Laughs weakly.*) I certainly don't want to intrude, Mrs. Washburn. But we tape all our hot-line calls and we do have a record of a call from you, Mrs. Washburn—do you remember making it?

MURIEL. (*Growing excited.*) A what? A tape? A tape of me? How dare you!

AILEEN. It's policy.

MURIEL. I—will not be spied upon. Not by the F.B.I., or t.v. monitors in the grocery store, or the school board, or—you. I will not be taped, and reduced to microfilm, like—somebody dead. (*Begins waving her hands.*) I am alive, I am not—that other. *I am alive, can't you see!*

AILEEN. (*To Stephanie.*) Is she always like this?

MURIEL. (*Furious.*) "She" is the cat's mother!

AILEEN. (*Edging away, yet trying to maintain some measure of authority.*) I—I'm sorry to upset you, Mrs. Washburn, but you *did* call our office—didn't you? With a complaint against a party you identified as your daughter?

MURIEL. (*To Stephanie, now stony-faced.*) Don't believe a word of it, Stevie—it's all a tissue of lies.

AILEEN. (*Doggedly.*) I only want to help, Mrs. Washburn. If ... there is any substance to your complaint.

MURIEL. Yes! The school board has been abusing me for years. Refused to believe me—took the word of pathological liars over mine. *I* ended up being called a racist —*I*!

AILEEN. (*Confused.*) Oh dear. But this present complaint—

MURIEL. Do I look like a person with a complaint? I'm in exemplary health. There were thirty-seven staples in my head but they're gone now.

AILEEN. (*Edging backward, as MURIEL advances.*) I— I do have a directive to interview you, and to arrange for a medical examination—

MURIEL. Nobody touches me! Nobody unclothes me! Ever again!

AILEEN. The—the county assumes all expenses.

MURIEL. (*Snaps her fingers.*) Ah—*I* got it.

AILEEN. Yes?

MURIEL. *I* understand your confusion, miss: you're in the wrong apartment. There's an old woman down on the third floor—she called you. She's the victim you want.

AILEEN. But *you* are Muriel Washburn—aren't you?

MURIEL. (*With bravado.*) Who's "Muriel"? I'm Mother.

(*LIGHTS out.*)

Scene 6

LIGHTS up, modified. Shortly after the preceding scene, at extreme stage left, in a segment of LIGHT cast by a single floor lamp, STEPHANIE and AILEEN STANLEY are conferring. Both Muriel's and Stephanie's bedrooms are dark.
STEPHANIE serves Aileen tea, etc.

STEPHANIE. (*In a strange, impersonal voice.*) It wasn't a brain tumor she had to have removed last winter, it was a "capillary angioma." She'd been having a headache and wouldn't tell me and finally had to tell me so I took her for tests and it turned out she'd had a minor hemorrhage ... they discovered she'd had two or three over the course of her life ... there was this accumulation of blood in her mid-brain that had to be removed. A tight little ball of capillaries. Mother said, "Oh boy I have my own private 'black hole.'"

AILEEN. She is what you'd call ... delusional.

STEPHANIE. I love Mother, I can't "institutionalize" her. She won't even allow a nurse in here, or a sitter, or ... anyone except me.

AILEEN. (*Cautiously.*) Oh but they're all like that. At first.

STEPHANIE. I love Mother. I am defined as ... as the person who loves her. (*Clearly.*) For each of us on earth is so defined, by who we love, and who loves us.

AILEEN. The things I see in my line of work! Oh, it's ... just tragic sometimes. I mean, you wouldn't believe how *sad*. Elderly people *do* get abused.

STEPHANIE. You say ... there is a tape of Mother's conversation with one of your staff members? It's ... a permanent record?

AILEEN. Oh dear yes, I'm afraid so. But our records are *Private*.

STEPHANIE. (*Awkwardly.*) Even if ... if her charges turn out to be ... delusional?

AILEEN. It's the law. (*Cheerfully.*) But don't worry, Stephanie, no one will ever know. (*A pause.*) Outside our office.

STEPHANIE. I see. (*A pause, then speaks in her impersonal voice, as if for the record.*) Mother is a woman of enormous energy and intelligence. She should have been something more ambitious than a junior high science teacher ... She did apply to graduate school, to study astrophysics, but it was 1935, women weren't wanted, I think in fact she showed up at Cal Tech demanding an interview and they ... laughed at her. (*Peculiar smile.*) Not that I blamed them, or anyone—Mother *can* be funny.

AILEEN. (*As if misunderstanding.*) Oh my yes—so witty! For a woman of her age.

STEPHANIE. Mother was such a popular teacher—for years. Her students loved her—she was so funny. Demanding, and—a disciplinarian—but fair. Then ... in the Sixties ... things began to shift. The school district, the population ... the racial mix. Mother tried to maintain the old ways but her students rebelled, some of them actually ... threatened her ... or she claimed they did. And the younger teachers weren't sympathetic. (*With more emotion.*) She was followed leaving the school building one day, she was knocked down on the street ... another time she was slashed with a razor. But the boy denied it, and ... (*With a resigned gesture.*) and there was such controversy ... the school board advised early retirement.

AILEEN. (*Too buoyant for situation.*) You'd never know she's had brain surgery! Gee whiz, some of those patients I see ... they're paralyzed, or aphasiac, or blind, or ... just plain *not there*. (*Pause; unintentional irony.*) Your mother would fit in real well in a good nursing home where there was, y'know, lots of activities. Social life. Muriel Washburn would be a real mover and shaker.

STEPHANIE. (*As if not hearing; bitter.*) ... Mother said the boy had a razor, he slashed her forearm, threatened to ... slash her throat. The boy said she'd cut herself on the edge of his locker! It was his word and his parents' and friends' against Mother's ... She never got over it.

(*Pause.*)

AILEEN. (*A sort of professional cheeriness.*) So, Stephanie—you're flying out to Denver tomorrow?

STEPHANIE. I ...intend to.

AILEEN. Give 'em hell! Wish I could come along.

STEPHANIE. (*Abstractly.*) What is real, what is invented ... the distinction isn't always clear. (*Pause.*) Mother used to tell us, Jill and me, that the way the stars "twinkle" is just an optical illusion. Delusion?—It's the movement of Earth's atmosphere, actually. The way the atmosphere bends light rays that causes it.

AILEEN. (*Self-absorbed.*) *I'm* thinking of quitting my job. The nasty things I see—the "Hot Line" cases—brrrrr!

STEPHANIE (*Slowly, as if just realizing.*) The eye invents so much. Especially in the Heavens.

AILEEN. (*Briskly picks up briefcase, prepares to leave.*) Well look—here's my card. Any time you need the name of a good registered nurse, or, y'know, just someone to watch over Muriel when you're away. Male nurses are great: even the gays have some muscle. And when it's time for the nursing home ... I know all the inside dope.

STEPHANIE. (*Staring at the card for a long pained moment.*) Oh. Thank you.

AILEEN. (*Shaking hands with Stephanie, at the door.*) Well! Stephanie Washburn! It's an honor to sit and chat with you—even in these circumstances.

STEPHANIE. (*Barely concealing her distaste; forced cordiality.*) Oh ... it was very nice to meet you. I'm just sorry about the—misunderstanding.

AILEEN. (*Cheerfully.*) No problem. About twenty percent of the calls we get are filed under the code "CUCKOO"—I mean, "delusional"—but we have to investigate them all. It's state law.

STEPHANIE. (*Trying to disguise how much this point means to her.*) And ... the tape can't be erased?

AILEEN. (*Nudging Stephanie, familiarly.*) Oh now "Stevie"—don't worry! Nobody's gonna leak classified information to the press!

(*AILEEN leaves. LIGHT fades to illuminate STEPHANIE, who stands frozen; insulted; an expression of cold fury on her face.*)

STEPHANIE. (*As the mask drops.*) I don't love anyone! Any of you! I mean you! I hate hate hate (*As SHE tears Aileen's card to bits and scatters the pieces.*) you all! (*Begins to pack a suitcase furiously.*) But I 'm going anyway.

(*LIGHTS out.*)

Scene 7

LIGHTS up. The following night. MURIEL, in the apartment alone, is speaking over the telephone. She wears her oversized sweater, pedal pushers, and jogging shoes; her turban is wrapped loosely around her head and affixed with a gaudy jeweled brooch.

Approximately four-fifths of the stage is now in an umbral darkness, converging on stage left, front, where MURIEL paces about in a circle of LIGHT cast by a floor lamp. SHE does a good deal of squinting and blinking, and, during this speech, several times presses her fingertips against her forehead or eyes, with a suggestion of pain, dizziness, or fatigue. But her voice is generally upbeat, ebullient.

A chair has been placed in front of the door as a sort of barricade.

MURIEL. (*Gaily.*) No no *no* I don't need anyone to stay with me. Stevie knows better than to try that again. (*Voice rising.*) *I don't need any caretaker, thank you. I'm of sound mind and body.* (*Relents somewhat.*) Well—I have my own friends. Yes. I have a ... a special friend. Yes: male. Tomorrow night is eclipse night and we're going out dancing. (*Girlish laughter.*) He's from an old Spanish family ... from Castellón de la Plana. What d'you mean, is he my age? (*Listens.*) Oh yes—she knows. Sure she's a wee bit jealous, but ... that's her problem. (*Excited.*) Tomorrow night is the lunar eclipse, the first time in seven years we'll be able to see an eclipse clearly in North America. Oh I can't wait! It will begin here about 9:20 P.M. and by 10:30 it should be at its fullest. The moon might be orangish, or dark red, depending ... on the earth's atmosphere: how discolored, I mean. Be sure the children see it, Jill? Promise? (*A bit too urgently.*) Jill? *Promise*?

(*From extreme stage right, STEPHANIE appears out of the darkness, in the corridor outside the Washburns' apartment. SHE is carrying her handbag, suitcase, and a small package under one arm. She is wearing an attractive belted trench coat but the belt is twisted in back; her hair is windblown; her eyes oddly bright. SHE walks with studied care as if mildly, and unaccustomedly, drunk.*)

MURIEL. (*Querulously.*) Jill, I'm having a hard time hearing you. I wonder if it's *you-know-who with their you-know-what* devices. (*Disguising her voice.*) There's a way of eluding the bastards, though! So they can't identify you on their tapes! (*Laughs.*)

(STEPHANIE has taken out her door key, fumbles fitting it into the lock, drops it. Stoops to pick it up but can't seem to find it in the dark.)

MURIEL. ... I *said* everything is fine. Hunky-dory, sweetie. I called 'cause I guess I been a sort of negligent mother ... these thirty-odd years. *(In a rush of feeling.)* I just want you to know I love you, honey. Love my two little girls more than anything on earth or ... anywhere. Remember that, honey, will you? *(Stricken with feeling, MURIEL touches her head, dislodges the turban which falls to the floor revealing her thin, short hair and the jagged scar in her scalp.)* Oh honey you know that—don't you? You and Stevie?

(STEPHANIE rings the DOORBELL. MURIEL freezes.)

MURIEL. ... It's the doorbell. *(Frightened, excited.)* But he's supposed to come tomorrow night, not tonight. It's too soon. I'm not ready. Oh God! *(Picks up the turban and tries to put it on, but it falls off again.)* 'Bye, honey!
    STEPHANIE. Mother? Are you there?

(MURIEL approaches the door cautiously.)

STEPHANIE. Mother? It's Stephanie. Open the door.
    MURIEL. It's ... who?
    STEPHANIE *(Impatiently.)* It's me. Your daughter Stephanie. I lost my key.
    MURIEL *(Alarmed.)* You're in Denver, Colorado. It's two hours earlier there. You can't be in two time zones simultaneously.
    STEPHANIE. Mother, don't *joke*. For God's sake don't *joke*. Just let me in.

MURIEL. Unless you're sub-atomic particles you can't be in two time zones simultaneously.

STEPHANIE. (*Half screaming.*) Damn it, let me in.

(*MURIEL pushes the chair away from the door; unbolts and unlocks the door; STEPHANIE steps inside, stumbles against the chair and almost falls. SHE drops her handbag, her suitcase, but hangs onto the package.*)

STEPHANIE. (*A mild drunken slur to her voice.*) What's this chair doing here?

MURIEL. It 's a barricade.

STEPHANIE. A what? I almost broke my neck. (*Squinting.*) Why's it so dark in here?

MURIEL. You aren't supposed to be here. (*Confused, alarmed.*) Why are you here? What day is it?

STEPHANIE. Why did you barricade the door? Did someone try to get in?

MURIEL. There was ... someone named Hugh. One of our neighbors, remember? Causing trouble. (*Presses her fingertips against her eyes.*) I refused to let the son of a bitch in.

(*STEPHANIE walks swaying to the circle of LIGHT, sits in a chair, legs outstretched. Her face looks flaccid, her eyes unnaturally bright.*
MURIEL shuts the door, locks and bolts it, and, grunting, pushes the chair back in place. STEPHANIE observes her without comment.)

MURIEL. You ... aren't supposed to be here. Is it my fault you're here?

(*STEPHANIE makes a gesture as if to indicate it doesn't matter.*)

MURIEL. Is it my fault ...?

(*STEPHANIE removes a pint bottle of Scotch from the paper bag, unscrews the top, carefully takes a swallow and wipes her mouth daintily with the back of her hand. SHE hiccups.*)

MURIEL. Oh! Shame on you! My own daughter ... reeling drunk.
STEPHANIE. (*With dignity.*) I am not reeling. I have never in my life ... *reeled.*
MURIEL. (*Guiltily, defensively.*) You flew to Denver on the six o'clock flight. You know you did.

(*STEPHANIE shrugs.*)

MURIEL. You ... didn't?

(*STEPHANIE shrugs again. Hiccups. SHE starts to unbutton her coat but fumbles and gives up; MURIEL comes to help her but SHE too is clumsy and can't force the buttons through the buttonholes.*)

MURIEL. Oh I won't be blamed! I won't be a ... scapegoat!
STEPHANIE. (*Dreamily.*) I watched the plane leave without me. No one is to blame.
MURIEL. But ... why? (*Angrily.*) They stopped you, didn't they? The airport police?
STEPHANIE. ... Sat in a cocktail lounge talking things over. In the inside of my head. (*Raps on her forehead with her knuckles; giggles.*) Just sat.
MURIEL. (*Muttering.*) There are t.v. monitors everywhere in that airport, it's so obvious they don't even

try to hide. You get X-rayed just walking minding your own damn business.

STEPHANIE. They can't see the inside of your head though.

MURIEL. Oh yes they can.

STEPHANIE. They *can't*. Not if you know how (*Giggles shrilly.*) to block 'em.

MURIEL. (*Disgusted.*) You're drunk. My own daughter—reeling *drunk.*

(*MURIEL secures the turban on her head, tries to tidy up both Stephanie and herself.*)

STEPHANIE. (*Drinking from the bottle.*) Oh Momma don't be mad at me, everybody's mad at me, I ... want to *die.* So *ashamed.* I called them and I told them, How can I leave my mother I told them, Momma isn't well and she needs me I told them (*Voice rising, childlike.*), nobody loves me like my Momma on this earth. (*A pause.*) Now they're mad at me 'cause I told the truth. (*A pause.*) Once in my Goddamn life I told the truth now they hate me. So *ashamed.*

MURIEL. Oh Stevie.

STEPHANIE. I don't care Momma, I told the truth for once. I can't leave *here.* (*At the word "here" STEPHANIE stamps her feet on the floor like a child in a tantrum.*)

(*MURIEL draws away, as if frightened.*)

MURIEL. (*To herself.*) They made a tape of this, they *know.*

STEPHANIE. (*Starts to cry, softly.*) I said out there, at the airport I was saying, maybe it's 'cause I saw some pilots walking by in their uniforms, y'know, I said, I want to see my father's picture just once. I have a right, I said.

MURIEL. (*Alarmed.*) Your father? What about him?

STEPHANIE. I was telling them, I have a right to see that man's *face*.

MURIEL. (*Guiltily.*) Dwight James Washburn walked out in 1957. He took his face with him forever.

STEPHANIE. I was his little girl but I can't remember.

MURIEL. Because the man was nothing special.

STEPHANIE. Yes he was, he was. You loved him once so he *was*. I want to see that for myself, Momma. (*Voice rising, pleading.*) Momma, I am thirty-eight years old.

(*MURIEL in a sudden fury of activity slams out of the living room, rummages around in her bedroom, snaps on the crooknecked bedside lamp. STEPHANIE watches blinking as SHE pulls out cartons from beneath her bed and out of a closet, tosses them about, etc. SHE is murmuring inaudibly to herself, "I won't be blamed, I won't be blamed." We see her actions through her opened door and through the transparent wall of her room.*
MURIEL reappears, triumphant, waving a glossy photograph.)

MURIEL. *I* will not be blamed.

(*STEPHANIE reaches for the photograph with a quavering hand. Her expression is open, hopeful, childlike.*)

STEPHANIE. (*Bringing the photograph to the light, squinting; after a pause.*) This is ... my father? (*STEPHANIE turns over the photograph, examines it all around, suspiciously. Flat, accusing voice.*) This ... is Errol Flynn.

MURIEL. So? I warned you he was nobody special.

(STEPHANIE gives a little scream, laughing or half-sobbing, and tears the photograph into tiny bits.
A pause. LIGHTS begin to fade. MURIEL gingerly approaches STEPHANIE to comfort her. Focus upon the couple MURIEL eases into the chair beside STEPHANIE, to embrace her; STEPHANIE, weeping, softly, presses her head against Muriel's breast.)

MURIEL. (*An improvised tune.*)
In the green of the year
When there's nothing to fear.
(SHE hums, stroking STEPHANIE's face and hair.)
In the green of the year
When there's nothing to fear.

STEPHANIE. I couldn't leave you, Momma. You know that.

MURIEL. Oh Stevie. I know, I know.

STEPHANIE. I love you, Momma. I'm right here.

MURIEL. But it isn't fair, honey. (*Strokes her face, hair.*) It isn't fair for you, honey. (*A pause.*) Stevie! "Stevie-the-bear": remember your teddy bear, honey, how you'd pretend *he* was Stevie when you went to bed? Remember, honey?

STEPHANIE. (*Quietly.*) No, Momma. I don't remember.

(LIGHTS out.)

Scene 8

DARKNESS: sultry tango MUSIC.
LIGHTS up: very dim light, as MURIEL (her identity at first unclear) moves about the living room lighting

candles. *These are unusually tall, elegant candles in silver candlestick holders placed strategically about the set. MURIEL moves to the tango beat, with obvious delight and anticipation.*

As LIGHT comes up, we see that MURIEL is wearing a new wig, a silvery-blond wig styled rather like the hairstyle made famous by Marilyn Monroe. Her dress is long, black, slinky, glamorous. In the soft mellow light SHE appears young, transformed, beautiful.

STEPHANIE has passed out in the chair, extreme stage left. SHE wakes, confused; shaking her head. The bottle, apparently empty, falls to the floor.

STEPHANIE. ... Mother? Where are you? (*Tries to stand, sinks back. SHE has a violent headache.*)

(*Stage right, in the shadows, are boxes filled with Muriel's belongings. There are a number of them, neatly stacked, perhaps shading off into the wings, We do not see the end of them.*)

STEPHANIE. ... Mother? (*Craning her neck, staring; at Muriel.*) Is that you?

(*As the tango continues, MURIEL performs a dance step, solo, facing the audience and STEPHANIE who seems to be paralyzed in her chair.*)

STEPHANIE. You'll ... injure yourself. You know you've fallen. Mother—*you know you've fallen.*

(*As SEÑOR RÍOS appears, stage right, in the corridor, approaching the front door of the apartment, MURIEL primps in a mirror; STEPHANIE becomes agitated, though incapable of rising from her chair.*)

STEPHANIE. He isn't coming, Mother! You know he isn't! You made it all up! You've invented everything! Your mind ... isn't right! You know it, and I know it!

(*SEÑOR RÍOS, flowers in hand, rings the bell. MURIEL hurries to answer it, trying to disguise her excitement.*)

STEPHANIE. There's nobody there! Your mind isn't right! Don't answer that door, Mother!

(*MURIEL opens the door, SEÑOR RÍOS enters. HE bows to her graciously, takes her hand and kisses it. He is a tall, even massive man; swarthy-skinned, with a handsome moustache; an old-fashioned courtliness to his bearing and manner. He wears a tuxedo with a red cummerbund and black, highly polished shoes.*
We hear near-inaudible murmurings. SEÑOR RÍOS speaks in Spanish; MURIEL seems almost to be singing or humming, interrupting herself frequently with bursts of light, girlish, tinkling laughter.
The flowers are orange gladioli, which MURIEL puts at once in a waiting vase.)

STEPHANIE. Don't touch them   Don't smell them! They're out of the garbage dumpster! Oh Momma, they're *poison!*

(*MURIEL and SEÑOR RÍOS whisper together, then begin to dance.*
THEY dance for perhaps a full minute, performing the tango flawlessly. It is an urgent, sensuous, romantic beat.)

STEPHANIE. Momma, you'll fall, you'll hurt yourself. You know you can't dance ... (*Agitated.*) Come to bed, Momma. Oh Momma, it's so late.

(*SEÑOR RÍOS escorts MURIEL to the door; the two are both affectionate and rather formal in their behavior. At the door, MURIEL suddenly remembers something.*)

STEPHANIE. Mother ...?

(*MURIEL tiptoes almost stealthily to Stephanie as if approaching a sleeping child's crib. SHE leans over her, kisses her. STEPHANIE raises her arms as if to retain her but cannot.*)

STEPHANIE. Mother, where are you going?

(*MURIEL returns to SEÑOR RÍOS links her arm through his, and the couple leaves through the front door. Tango MUSIC ends.*)

STEPHANIE. (*Her voice a high thin wail, trailing off to silence*) Mother ...!

(*A beat or two then LIGHTS OUT.*)

APPENDIX

Notes for Stephanie's speech, as she rehearses.

... Politics is like war, let us admit it, but there is hope in unity ... a hope whose name is "feminism" ... the "women's movement" ... though the hope is at all times imperiled ... at the present time especially so.

... Women's political perspective ... the only vital

... Deep skepticism among youth ... (male) graft in politics, business ... (male) corruption ... (male) violations of ethical standards ... The Senate ... Speaker of the House ... former Presidents ... business leaders ...

... Our enemies fear us ... the anti-abortion forces ...

... After years of struggle, women's income in America is only 75% of men's for equal work ...

... must unite: FEMINISM is the ONLY WAY OF THE FUTURE.

COSTUME PLOT

Muriel - Scene 1

Purple sweatshirt with logo on back; Blue t-shirt; Multi-color crazy print knit stretch pants; Green check wool man's coat with mismatched buttons; Short red wig; Tube socks with blue stripes; Light blue tennis shoes.

Muriel - Scene 2

Lose: coat, add: white robe w/elbow patches; Lose: wig add: turban; Keep same top, pants and shoes from Scene 1.

Muriel - Scene 3

Same as Sc. 2.

Muriel - Scene 4

Lose: robe and turban, add short red wig and one red glove and one blue glove.

Muriel - Scene 5

Lose: top, socks and sneakers; add: blue polyester dress with bow and button front and grey wig.

Muriel - Scene 6

No change.

Muriel - Scene 7

Remove t-shirt, add: bra, lose: pants; add: robe (same); lose grey wig, add: turban; add: socks and sneakers (same); underdress black tights.

Muriel - Scene 8

Lose: everything but bra; add: 40's black, beaded crepe dress; black heels; platinum wig.

Stephanie - Scene 1

Beige wool skirt w/belt; Blue patterned blouse; Panty hose; Checked tan and brown riding jacket; Olive trench coat; Brown pumps; Gold earrings and pin; Watch.

Stephanie - Scene 2

Lose: jacket.

Stephanie - Scene 3
No change.
Stephanie - Scene 4
Add: sweater.
Stephanie - Scene 5
No change.
Stephanie - Scene 6
No change.
Stephanie - Scene 7
Lose: sweater, add: trench coat.
Stephanie - Scene 8
Add trench coat.
Aileen - Scenes 5 & 6
Black pleated pants; White blouse with black lines and bow; Black and white lined jacket; Light blue London Fog raincoat; Black loafers with small heel; Black earrings; Gold chain necklace; Watch; Glasses.

Property   Plot

apartment key on string
grocery bag #2
misc. grocery items
3 receipts, 1 per bag
hanky
mango
anchovies
gouda cheese, in pkg.
pink stationery
vase
paper towel
executive folder
afghan
2 cans of beer
2 spoons
suitcase
sm. ringed binder
9 manilla folders
(2) teacups and saucers
keys
cardboard box
single candle
(4) pillar candlesticks
packing boxes
single glad. stem

grocery bag #1
grocery bag #3
seafood combo
misc. dry cleaning
gourmet chocolate box
jar o' shrimp
bar of soap, wrapped
caviar
pencil
wilted orange glads
pillow
pencil
towel
qt. of ice cream
more pink stationery
briefcase
pen
business card
pint of scotch w/cap
kitchen chair
photo of Errol Flynn
holder for above
candles
matches

Furniture

sofa w/pillows	shelf unit w/ stereo equip. & books on shelves, phone, appt./address book on top
t.v. and stand adjacent to shelves	rug
coffee table w/space & feminist books	sofa table w/long corded, sturdy lamp; ledger and stapler in drawer
rocker (Muriel's chair)	standing lamp (behind rocker)
SR armchair	sm. table behind armchair w/long corded lamp
Stephanie's bed	Stephanie's dresser w/phone, lamp, tissues, mirror
Muriel's bed w. afghan	Muriel's chest w/lamp and photos on top
Muriel's mirror	Muriel's wig stand
3 door units	2 ceiling pieces
nebula painting	

THE ECLIPSE

SCENE DESIGN
"IN DARKEST AMERICA"

FULL MIRROR
WIG ON STAND
SM. CHEST W/ GOOSENECK LAMP
HEAD
MURIEL'S BED
SEATS
TABLE W/ LAMP

ENTRY HALL OF APT. BLDG.
NEBULA ABOVE W/ LIGHT (MOVING SHADOW)
FLY ON CTR. SHEER
SOFA TABLE W/ LAMP
SOFA W/ PILLOWS
COFFEE TABLE
8X10 ORIENTAL RUG
ARM CHAIR
T.V. SET
LOW BOOK CASE W/ BOOKS
SEATS

DRESSING TABLE W/ TELEPHONE
MIRROR
TABLE LAMP
STEPHANIE'S BED
HEAD
SEATS
MURIEL'S CHAIR
ARCHING FLOOR LAMP
TO KITCH.

TONE CLUSTERS

SCENE DESIGN
"IN DARKEST AMERICA"

12' x 14' PROJECTION SCREEN

6' x 8'
PROJECTION
SCREEN ABOVE
AUDIENCE
HEAD

6' x 8'
PROJECTION
SCREEN ABOVE
AUDIENCE
HEAD

T.V.
MONITOR

T.V.
MONITOR

T.V.
MONITOR

360° SWIVEL
CHAIRS

(3) PROJECTORS
ABOVE

J.T.P.

PROJECTORS (3) ABOVE